SHERLOCK HOLMES

The Breath *of* God

SHERLOCK HOLMES

The Breath of God

GUY ADAMS

TITAN BOOKS

Sherlock Holmes: The Breath of God
Print edition ISBN: 9780857682826
E-book edition ISBN: 9780857686008

Published by
Titan Books
A division of Titan Publishing Group Ltd
144 Southwark St
London
SE1 0UP

First edition: September 2011
10 9 8 7 6 5 4 3 2

Names, places and incidents are either products of the author's imagination or used fictitiously. Any resemblance to actual persons, living or dead (except for satirical purposes), is entirely coincidental.

Visit our website: www.titanbooks.com

What did you think of this book? We love to hear from our readers. Please email us at: readerfeedback@titanemail.com, or write to us at the above address.

To receive advance information, news, competitions, and exclusive offers online, please sign up for the Titan newsletter on our website: **www.titanbooks.com**

A CIP catalogue record for this title is available from the British Library.

Printed and bound in the USA.

To Phil Jarrett, my Watson

CHAPTER ONE

THE DEATH OF HILARY DE MONTFORT

I was not there, let me be clear on that point.

When presenting the career of my friend Sherlock Holmes to the reading public, I have most commonly recounted events as one who saw them with his own eyes. The one obvious exception being the accounts of his many clients. Even then – perhaps *especially* then – I have repeated their testimonies as close to verbatim as my notes will allow. Whether Holmes will credit it or not (and he does not) I have always considered it important in these sketches to present nothing less than the pure truth. Enlivened in tone perhaps, constructed with a wish to excite as well as inform, but never altered in detail.

When looking to how this affair started – an affair that would see London in chaos mere moments before this brave new century began – I can only look to the eyewitness reports gathered by the constabulary, the effusive reportage of the press and the colour and clarity offered by hindsight.

But, whether I was there or not, whether I can swear to each and every event in those last moments of the life of Hilary De Montfort (for, as is so often the way, our story began in death), begin here we must. Because when the Breath of God first blew, it blew on young De Montfort, socialite and expender of other people's bank accounts.

And it blew so very, *very* hard.

De Montfort commenced the evening of the 27th of December 1899, with champagne and cards. He ended it in a broken heap in the middle of Grosvenor Square. As for what came in-between, I will tell you as well as I can. Certainly it involved a great deal of running for his life...

London is many cities in one, from the tarry reek of Rotherhithe and its opium houses, to the crisp refinement of Mayfair. Travelling its length and breadth in the pursuit of Holmes' enquiries I would often find myself faced with the most spectacular sights. I have travelled halfway across the world, lain bleeding on a foreign field of battle and yet the place most capable of filling me with awe is the city in which I now make my home. For that reason alone I don't believe I could live anywhere else.

For Hilary De Montfort I suspect London was a more singular place. His life revolved around club pursuits and fashionable addresses. In this he was not unusual amongst the youth of society's elite. His family had owned a considerable portion of Sussex for generations and until young Hilary found himself in line for familial duty and the responsibilities of running the estate, his time – and parents' money – was his own.

On the evening in question he had been ensconced at the tables of Knaves, one of the many gambling clubs to have opened since the demise of Crockford's forced gentlemen to take their money

and betting books elsewhere. He was by no means a bad gambler, as likely to leave the tables with another man's fortune as he was to lose his own. That night the cards had been dealt in his favour and the doorman – a dour gent by the name of Langford – would later remark on the young man's high spirits as he left the club.

"He was as fizzy as champagne," Langford was quoted as saying in the *The Daily News*. "He skipped down the front steps as full of life as any that was."

It was to be a short-lived condition.

Snow had begun to fall earlier that evening, and it was through swirling sheets of it that De Montfort made his way, on foot, to his next destination – the lounge of Salieri's, that week's preferred watering hole for young men with money to burn. Why he chose to walk given the inclement weather, we can only guess. Perhaps he hoped the cool air would clear his head of the excesses of Knaves; brush away the alcohol and cigar smoke, ready for him to absorb yet more.

When next we catch a glimpse of De Montfort, he is running in terror along the streets surrounding Grosvenor Square. He was spotted by an elderly gentleman making his own way home. The fellow was alerted to De Montfort by the sound of the young man's cries, constant and desperate, thrown over his shoulder as he hurled himself along the snow-covered pavement. It is clear that De Montfort believed himself to be pursued, though the ageing witness would swear an oath to Scotland Yard that the street had been empty but for the two of them.

"Hardly surprising when one considers the weather," he said to Inspector Gregson in his statement. "Not just the snow, though that was thick enough, but the wind which had built from little more than a breeze at the commencement of my journey to a veritable tornado at the close of it."

Gregson noted a considerable unease in the gent as he recalled the gale: "I had to grasp the street railings," he continued, "or for sure I would have been blown along the pavement after the poor young man. For some moments I was quite unable to see a thing, the snow whipped so thick it obscured all but the faint glow of the lamps above."

"And by the time it cleared...?" Gregson asked.

"There was no sign of him, the street was empty but for the snow drifts the wind left in its wake."

Indeed the peculiar patterns of the snow were remarked upon by the officer first attending the scene after De Montfort's body was discovered. The constable in question – a young chap by the name of Wilson, fresh in the job and quite thrilled to have "such a corker" of a cadaver on his patrol – was so impressed by the drifts of snow that he attempted to make a sketch of them in his notebook.

"It was as if the hand of God itself were on his heels," he would later say to Holmes. "Cutting its way across the square right after him. I reckon as it would take something of the sort to make that mess of him, he'd been worked over good and proper that's for sure."

Indeed he had. The damage was clearly beyond the work of a single individual. There was scarcely a bone left intact in his body, the flesh of which was purple and black with bruising. He was of the state expected of those unfortunates washed up on the banks of the River Thames, a bloated and disfigured approximation of a body. Of the weapon that caused such distress we could barely guess. There was no obvious impressions left on the remains, not the mark of a club or cudgel. I might have sworn that the body had fallen from a great height. But as varied as our capital might be, it will always be found wanting of mountain ranges. This man had died in the clear, open space of one of London's garden squares, and there was little to explain the state of his remains

CHAPTER TWO

THE PSYCHICAL DOCTOR

"I simply cannot credit it, Watson!" my friend shouted, offering that theatrical sweep of his arms with which he loved to embellish his loudest announcements. "How can a man of science, a rational thinker, a man with both feet pressed sensibly on the ground, even consider believing in such poppycock?"

"I didn't say I believed it," I replied, lighting my pipe and flinging the match into the fire, "simply that one should approach everything with an open mind."

"Open...?" Holmes rolled his eyes and slumped back in his armchair. "There is no other expression so capable of filling me with dread as that. An *open mind*... how can one even begin to consider it? An open mind in this sea of detritus... It would be like swimming along the Thames with one's mouth gaped wide, swallowing mouthful upon mouthful of effluvia..."

"You have said yourself that it is a mistake to theorise without data. That a good detective simply absorbs all the information and then deduces accordingly."

"All the *relevant* information," Holmes countered. "One must trust in one's sense of logic and rationality to filter out the dross. A mind is not elastic, it cannot simply be filled with shovel after shovel of meaningless nonsense. Data must be gathered carefully, selectively, so that an accurate picture can be formed."

"And your picture of our prospective client?"

Holmes flung the man's card onto the dining table and took up watch by the window. "Time will tell, but logic dictates he is either charlatan or fool."

I sighed but could see little point in continuing the argument, my friend's opinions were not readily changed. The card was for Dr John Silence, whose reputation – though not company – was familiar to me. Indeed, there was scarcely a medical man in London that cannot have heard of the self-labelled "Psychical Doctor". He was a man of means – though nobody could say where it was that he had gained his money – who offered treatment to those who couldn't afford it. Many of my profession, myself included, had been known to put a few hours in at the workhouses, or wherever our services might be best received, but most of us scarcely had the finances to make it the lion's share of our workload.

Dr Silence was also much discussed for reasons other than his generosity. In recent years, he had shifted his focus away from the purely physical aspects of medicine to concentrate on what he termed "psychic illness". It was a source of much discussion amongst medical circles as to what he might mean by that expression. His talk of "demonic possession" and "intrusion from beyond the earthly realms" did little for his reputation (and indeed engendered precisely the sort of response evidenced by my colleague, a man thoroughly wedded to a rational view of the world). There were some, however, who saw his work as an extension of the alienist's art.

However it may be dressed up, there was clear evidence of people who had benefited from Silence's attentions. But then, Holmes would argue that many who visited so-called clairvoyants would leave after an hour's theatre feeling emboldened by the experience, this was not to say the charlatan in question should be encouraged.

I was also sceptical, and yet the reports of Dr Silence's character were so respectable I found it hard not to offer at least a sliver of consideration towards his practices. I would meet the man and have him explain his business before choosing to judge him. Holmes appeared to have no such inclination. At least he had agreed to an appointment, if nothing else his curiosity might be relied upon to secure that much of his time.

Holmes had been in a foul mood for some months, something Mrs Hudson, our landlady, was quick to tell me on my return. After marrying Mary I had, of course, taken my leave of these shared rooms. After her untimely passing, however, loneliness – and in truth a need to tighten the purse strings – had seen me return. It was clear that Mrs Hudson believed the lack of my calming influence in that intervening period was what had seen Holmes' mood descend to these all-time lows. In truth I had never been able to control him, he would be who he would be, his mood as changeable and easily shifted as a boat cast out onto the ocean. One thing I can claim the responsibility for is the change in his professional circumstances, though it was not a change for the better. As the nineteenth century drew to a close it brought with it the last gasp of his consulting business. Within a few short years he would retire – retreating, against all prediction, to a life of rural comfort in Sussex – but those last years saw his time constantly bombarded with cases he considered beneath his attention. He had always been dismissive of my attempts to bring his work before a larger public, and time would eventually give him a solid reason for doing so. His practice had become so renowned that special arrangements were struck with the postal service to handle the quantity of mail he received. Much of it bore no case at all, from threats to job applications, erstwhile biographers (no doubt of the opinion that they could do a better job of it than I) to proclamations of love.

The latter was particularly common and never ceased to amaze me. Had I not made clear that Holmes, while not blind to the attractive qualities of women, never sought them for his own? Many a slanderous wag has attempted to suggest this was because his tastes lay in a different direction, in fact he simply possessed no interest in the subject whatsoever. Holmes was not a man of the body – as evidenced by how poorly he treated his own – he was a man of the mind, and no amount of cologne-drenched poetry by the first post would change the fact.

His morning routine had been to sit cross-legged before the fire, the smoke of discarded love letters and other dross combining with that of his post-breakfast pipe, as he winnowed down the correspondence to letters that at least held some professional content. A second pass would then sift those of some interest from the usual missing persons and suspicious husbands (of the former he had long since given up being able to satisfy the countless families that found their number lacking, people vanished every day and most of them didn't want to be found).

So it was with some surprise to me that Dr Silence's enquiry saw him pass through both postal stages to reach that most hallowed of positions: the appointment. Though by the time he appeared to claim it, Holmes' mood had sunk even further. A few hours of unsatisfactory chemistry had seen him drape himself over the chaise, dangling his acid-stained hands by his side as he sucked on cigarette after cigarette, looking for all the world like a prone steam engine wrapped in a threadbare dressing gown.

"A guest, sir," said Billy, Holmes' page, at the due hour. "A Dr John Silence, 'e claims to 'ave an appointment."

Holmes simply growled and flung what remained of his cigarette towards the fireplace. It fell short and had added yet another black wound to the rug by the time I reached it and extinguished it.

"Do send him up, Billy," I replied, determined that one of us at least should show the man some civility on his arrival.

Doctor Silence was not as I had imagined, there was nothing showy or "mystical" about his appearance. He was in his late thirties, thin and with an immaculately trimmed beard. His dress was suitably formal yet not in the least ostentatious, an outfit designed to match his environment rather than draw attention. He appeared urbane, yet my exposure to Holmes' methods were such that I automatically glanced at the knees of his trousers and discerned a dusting of animal hair. Light and short, too thick to be a cat so a likely sign that Silence owned a domesticated dog. He also had on a pair of new shoes, the lack of creasing in the leather could not simply be down to the attention of a decent valet.

I noticed Holmes glance at the man, no doubt taking in all that I had observed and more, before returning his attention to his cigarette case which was distressingly empty.

"Good morning," Holmes muttered, waving towards an empty chair but making no effort to shake the man's hand. He vanished instead towards the bookshelves, on the hunt for more cigarettes.

"Morning," Silence replied, looking towards me as the only man in the room willing to make a civil effort.

"John Watson," I said, shaking his hand and repeating Holmes' direction to sit down.

"Ah," Silence nodded, settling into the armchair, "I've heard of you, of course."

"All of London has heard of Watson," Holmes agreed, pulling a set of shipping timetables from the shelf so that he could reach the small brown parcel behind them, "his popular writings have seen to that."

"Well, indeed," Silence admitted, "though I did mean in a professional capacity. We shared the same anatomy professor at Barts."

"Really?" I laughed, while Holmes tore at the brown paper of his tobacco order. "You learned under Bloodthirsty Barrow too, did you?"

Silence smiled and nodded. "And like you, I dare say, I winced at the pleasure he seemed to take in each and every cut."

I turned to Holmes. "It wouldn't surprise me in the least were Sir Lionel Barrow to have crossed your path Holmes, there was certainly a homicidal air to him."

My friend shrugged and put a cigarette to his lips. "The name means nothing." He exhaled a large mouthful of smoke that partially obscured his bored face. "Perhaps I should give the two of you some privacy in which to... *chat*?" The half-tone of disgust he gave that last word was not lost on me. There was nothing smaller to Holmes than small talk.

"Forgive me," Silence said, "but as much as it's a pleasure to find you in Dr Watson's company, it is your attention that I was hoping for."

"You have it," Holmes replied, reclining once more upon the chaise. "But only because of the singular evidence of the Labrador hair on your trouser shins."

Silence glanced down and began to pick off the hair. "Most observant of you," he said. "Though I fail to see its relevance."

"You are clearly as fastidious as a cat in your appearance," Holmes answered. "The fact that you've travelled here without once taking note of the state of your trousers suggests to me that your mind is greatly occupied. It is a condition of which I am extremely envious so I lie here in the hope it might be contagious."

"I can assure you I have an incredible story to relate. You may be aware that I am not in the habit of consulting others, in point of fact I'm rather more comfortable as the one consulted."

"I am aware – by reputation at least – of your practice, though it would be dishonest of me to suggest I approve of it."

Silence smiled. "I seek nobody's approval, Mr Holmes, and time will tell if you maintain your views."

Holmes waved the thought away, as if it were so impossible that his opinion could shift that it was scarcely worth mentioning. In truth though I had noted a change in his behaviour. For all of his outward show of disinterest – even disdain – he was attentive to every detail of the doctor's tale, indeed, by its conclusion he was rapt with attention.

CHAPTER THREE

SILENCE'S ACCOUNT

"It can scarcely surprise you," said our guest, "that scepticism is a common response to my work. Indeed, when discussing my practice, the only thing more potent and freely offered than derision is the gratitude of those few I am fortunate to be able to help. That the balance is thus maintained explains why I find it easy to rise above my detractors. Besides, far from being – as most of my critics believe – intangible, irrational theories and practices, the tenets of my work are deeply researched and honed. I dedicated five years of my life to expanding what I had been taught about the body to include what I could also learn of the spirit. I studied all over the world, from the ashrams alongside the Sabarmati River to the temples that lie in the most inhospitable regions of Tibet."

"My friend also has some knowledge of Tibet," I interjected, hoping that this might be the foundation for some mutual respect between client and detective.

"Knowledge is not valued by its geographical location," Holmes said, "rather by intellectual worth." He dismissed my interruption with a wave of his hand. "Please, Dr Silence, if we could progress beyond *justification* into the realm of *information*. Tell me what it is that you wish me to investigate."

"Very well, though I am less a potential client than a messenger, as you shall soon see.

"My medical practice has dwindled over the last year or two. I find that my esoteric services are in more demand and I must dedicate an increasing amount of my time to them. However, yesterday I was visited by an old medical patient, a sailor I had treated after an accident amongst the rigging had threatened to rob him of his left leg."

Silence then launched into his tale:

"Simcox," I greeted him, noting a slight limp to his stride but no more than might be expected given the cold this winter. "I trust your old infirmity has not returned?"

"Indeed not, Doctor," he replied, "these old bones are stronger than ever, it is for the sake of another that I call. You remember my Elsa?"

Elsa was his daughter, a bonny-faced thing that had hung at my elbow throughout my earlier visits to the Simcox household, equally full of concern and fascination at my work. "Indeed," I assured him, "what ails the poor girl?"

"I only wish I knew, sir," he replied and with that he dropped into a chair and began to sob. It was clear that this stolid man had spent a considerable time strung as tight as one of his own sails. Now he was here, and hopeful of my relieving him of his strain, that strength was gone. I

poured him a brandy from the decanter on the sideboard – we doctors know that sometimes the most beneficial medicines are the simplest – and forced him to drink it before he attempted any further explanation.

"Forgive me, Doctor," he said finally, "the last few days have been more than I could stand. For a moment there, the weight of them quite overtook me."

"No need for apologies," I assured him. "I only hope I might help. Pray tell me all."

"It began a week or so ago," he explained, "in the early hours of the morning when my wife and I were asleep. I had been ashore for a couple of days, and had been enjoying the feel of solid ground beneath me. I am often away from home, of course, such is the lot of my profession, but I try and make the most of the time I do have and we had spent the day at the park, a few games, a packed hamper." He gave a full, warm smile at the memory. "We had leisured like gentry. But that night, with the sound of my Elsa's happy laughter still fresh in my ears, I awoke to find her screaming from her cot, as if the very devil himself had his nails in her. And perhaps, after all, he did...

"I was straight from my bed with my beloved Sally a mere hair behind me as we both ran to where our daughter lay. She was sat upright, the bed linen clutched in her fists as if she wished to tear it apart. Her eyes were fixed to a point on the ceiling where, look as I might, I could see nothing. Visible to me or not, it was clear that Elsa believed something to be there. 'Can you not see it squirm?' she asked before her eyes rolled back in their sockets and she passed out.

"I don't mind telling you, Doctor, I thought she was done for. I have seen my fair share of death on the waves, oceans claim their number year on year and there's not a man who has worked them that hasn't seen death. In that moment, when my daughter fell slack in my arms, I was quite sure that all life had vanished from her, so light, so insubstantial was she as I held her face towards the candlelight, desperate for sign of breathing. No sooner had I convinced myself she was gone but she stiffened in my arms and opened her eyes.

"'Daddy?' she asked, as if unsure for a moment who it was that held her.

"'That it is, my love,' I assured her, 'your mam and I are right here and there's nothing to be afeared of.' She smiled at that and, God help me, I've wondered since if that were the first sign of trouble.

"We laid her back in her bed and returned to sleep, putting it down as nothing more than a dream on her part. It wasn't until the following night that we were disillusioned of that fact.

"Again, it was long after my wife and I had fallen asleep that Elsa's attack came – yes, 'attack', I can think of no other word for it... We were woken by the sound of her cries and drew to her bedside in time to see her dash from the mattress and leap towards the ceiling of her room. I ran forward, eager to catch her before she fell, but imagine my surprise, Doctor, when she did no such thing. Her fingers

adhered to the dry plaster above us as she pulled herself along towards the shadows in the corner of her small room. 'It runs!' she cried. 'It tries to escape! I will have it! I will!' She smacked at the ceiling as if trying to grind imaginary spiders beneath her palms.

"'Elsa!' Sally cried, unable to bear the sight of our daughter in such impossible circumstances. 'Elsa!'

"She stopped pounding at the ceiling and slowly turned her head towards us. Doctor, I know the face of my own child, so I trust you will believe me when I say that the face that looked down at me from the shadows of the eaves was most certainly not hers. It was a shining, waxy thing, a grinning mask of teeth and sweat, an evil face, Doctor, the face of whatever it was that had – in that moment – possessed my girl as its own.

"My wife screamed and I may well have joined her, in truth I cannot remember. I will admit that the memory of that night is more than enough to make such a noise swell within my breast even now.

"At the sound of my wife's cry, Elsa returned to her own body. Her face softened in the light of the candles and her fingers lost whatever infernal magic they had possessed as she fell from the ceiling, dropping into my arms as I stepped beneath her.

"Oh but how she burned, Doctor! Her whole body gave off the heat of hot coals. Indeed, for a moment my instinct was to drop her lest my own skin be singed. I took her back to her bed, making a face at my wife to stop her cries. I didn't blame her for the reaction, but at that moment I wanted nothing more than for my daughter to return to sleep. I needed her to be normal again, to draw a veil over what we had seen.

"I tucked her in and pulled my wife back to the doorway. Little Elsa made no fuss at all, she looked for all the world like a girl who had just roused from an unusual dream, perhaps in her head that's all it was. Within a few minutes she was sleeping soundly and my wife and I withdrew to talk.

"We'd heard of your more recent work, Doctor, having always held you in esteem after you saved me my livelihood. I'll confess that some of the stories we heard sounded unbelievable. Even then, sir, believe me when I say we never doubted your reputation, just wondered whether exaggeration had crept into the telling. I mean, some of those stories..."

"I have lived an interesting life of late," I assured him, "whether the particular stories you heard were true or not I couldn't say but rest assured I have seen enough not to dismiss your account." At this reassurance he showed a considerable relief.

"Even with all I've heard," he admitted, "I half expected you to laugh in my face."

"Not a bit of it," I insisted. "In fact, if you will give me a moment to grab my hat and coat I will return with you to see your daughter myself right away."

The gratitude in his eyes was considerable. It will not surprise you when I say that I have seen that look many times in my profession, the first step in helping these unfortunates is often simply believing their stories.

I took the liberty of flagging down a hansom, time was of the essence and while my companion may not be accustomed to such decadent travel I am lucky enough to have the means.

"I rarely travel by anything else," interrupted Holmes.

Silence gave a small smile. "I forgot, you do charge for your services don't you? As you know I give my skills freely."

"You get what you pay for," muttered my friend, lighting another cigarette, "and my time is deemed precious."

"Then let us waste no more of it," Silence replied. "I shall continue...?" Holmes nodded impatiently.

We made our way to Simcox's rooms, the lower portion of a house near King's Cross.

The child was in her bed, despite the hour, and barely moved to acknowledge me as I entered with her father.

"Here he is," said Simcox to his wife. "Didn't I say he'd help?"

"You did," she smiled at me, "and I never doubted it. Thank you for coming, Doctor."

"A pleasure," I assured her, stooping down at the girl's bedside. Even when the supernatural is suspected, I commence my investigation from a medical standpoint. Partially this is habit, but neither am I so blind a believer as to ignore the possibility of a rational explanation. A number of times I have been called to such cases of possession – for that was certainly what Simcox's tale inferred – only to find clear medical reasons for such behaviour. Fever brings delirium and all manner of terrifying things may be uttered in the height of such a condition.

"But such things could hardly account for her climbing across the ceiling," I said.

"Indeed not," Silence agreed. "But then nothing natural could."

"No," agreed Holmes. "If it happened exactly as Simcox described, it is indeed inexplicable. But please, continue... Unless you have another engagement?" Holmes had noticed the doctor glance briefly towards the clock on our mantel.

"You may feel we both have," the doctor replied, "though there is more than enough time as yet."

There was no fever in Elsa. Other than a faint sheen of dust on her palms – which I took to be from her, as you say, quite inexplicable journey across the ceiling – she gave no outward sign of the experiences her father had described.

The medical examination thus satisfied, I progressed towards my more specialised area of expertise. I have, over the years, gathered a number of tools to facilitate my work. While much of what is commonly termed "the supernatural" takes place on a mental level, there are certain physical objects which I have found can help. Aids to concentration, herbs to engender a receptive state, crystals that may be used to focus certain energies... It was the latter that I retrieved from my bag, a small, opal-coloured gem given to me by a Dutch medium that I spent some months training with.

The stone is intended to draw out spirits, to attract them from wherever they may have become entrenched so that the perceptive psychic may pin them down.

At this explanation I noticed Holmes roll his eyes. Whether Silence caught the gesture or not he continued regardless.

I placed the stone on the child's forehead, stroking her cheek gently and reassuring her that all would soon be well – a somewhat overconfident statement I'll admit, but I wished to put the poor girl at ease.

I began an incantation which I often use in such circumstances. It's a simple little rhyme, nothing inherently spiritual, but as an aid to clearing the mind, I have found it most effective.

After only a few moments a change in the girl was obvious: her eyelids fluttering and her lips moving slowly as if trying to shape words but too tired to manage.

I placed my fingers on the crystal and immediately she fixed me with a stare that was so intense and so malevolent that I froze, utterly unsure of myself.

"Hello, Doctor," she said, her voice recognisably Elsa's and yet deeper, distorted. It was as if she were an old lady, the soft childish tones destroyed by years of abuse. "How good of you to visit."

I don't mind admitting that, while I have been in a number of situations where I consider my soul to have been in peril, there was something in that voice, a tinge of amusement perhaps, that made me more afraid than I can ever remember. From the soft, innocent face of this child I was observed by eyes immeasurably older than my own. I had attended that girl's bedside with a view to helping her, at that moment it felt as if it were I that was in need of assistance. I was a man considerably out of his depth and it took no more than those few words and the eyes of the being that said them to alert me to the fact.

"To whom am I speaking?" I asked, not expecting an answer – names are power in this alternative science, gentlemen – but wishing to clarify the fact that I was aware that the creature I was addressing was no young child.

The girl smiled and, again, it was an old smile, the sort of smile an adult would give to a young child who has just committed an amusing, precocious act.

"You know better than that, Doctor," she said, "though I have names to give you, none of them shall be my own."

"Names?" I asked.

She nodded, then tilted her head back, teeth clenching as if in some state of ecstasy. The young girl's skin rippled, as if fingers moved beneath it, caressing her bones. I feared for the girl terribly then, quite sure that this thing had no intention of leaving her alive once its game was done. Its attention snapped back to me.

"Yes," she – no, it – continued, "three names: the first is Hilary De Montfort, the second is the Laird of Boleskine, the third is Sherlock Holmes."

"Ha!" My friend leapt to his feet, pulling a thin trail of smoke across the room as he returned to the bookcase. "It asked for me by name did it? My reputation has spread far indeed if it's known even in the depths of Hell."

"Given the number of souls you have sent there in your time," Silence replied, "it doesn't surprise me at all."

Holmes was riffling through his collection of gazetteers and reference books. "Don't mind me," he muttered, running his fingers down indexes and flipping through pages, "pray continue."

"There is not much left to tell," Silence admitted.

Against all my expectations, having delivered the names, the girl convulsed and the creature's influence lifted. The crystal, which had glowed faintly with the charge of energy, extinguished, and the girl relaxed back in her bed.

"Elsa?" her mother asked. Both parents had held back while I had examined their daughter but I waved them forward now. There was no doubt in my mind that Elsa was once more herself. What I did not know – and still do not – was what was so important about those three names that a creature of such power would possess this child simply to pass them on. There was to be one more clue offered, but that came after I had taken my leave of Simcox and his family, reassuring him that his daughter was now free of whatever force had held her.

I stepped back onto those bustling streets around the railways. An area of constant movement filled with infernal noise: the rattle of rolling stock, the screech of steam whistles, the carnival jollity of the street organ and ribald song that pours as inevitably from the many public houses as the singers once their pockets are emptied. It is an alien place that quarter, a world in which the laws and opinions of gentlemen are rarely sought. I confess therefore that I was somewhat on edge as I made my way towards the station. There seemed to me to be an awareness in the eyes of those around me that one moved amongst them who did not belong. There was a feeling of hostility, of intense observation, marking my every step towards the platforms of St Pancras. I confess I nearly changed my plans and hailed a hansom. Certainly I would have done so were it not for the mocking voice in my head that pointed out – quite truthfully – that I had faced demons from Hell itself and yet was now nervous upon the side streets of my own home city.

I should not have doubted my own senses, they are sharper than many a man's and particularly attuned to the unearthly. I walked those streets with more than just my fellow men, a fact that soon became obvious when I noticed that everyone I passed was staring at me. I raised my hand to my face, assuming there was something about my appearance that had drawn curiosity. Glancing in the reflection of a shop window, it became clear there was nothing about me that veered from the norm. Nonetheless their attention clung, the heads of every single man, woman and child turning to watch me as I passed.

"There is something that interests you?" I asked of a gentlemen close to me. He was an elderly fellow with rheumy eyes and a reek of alcohol. He simply smiled and those dull eyes of his took on a sharper glint. I recognised in them the amused and utterly alien personality that had gazed out from young Elsa's eyes. "I see you!" I whispered. "I see you and call you out!"

All around me the invading personality began to laugh, from hoarse cackles in ageing breasts to the high-pitched giggles of infants, it borrowed every pair of lungs on that street for its own expression of amusement. It was an act of the most infernal puppetry I have ever seen and I felt certain my time had come.

"Beware the Breath of God, Doctor!" it shouted, a chorus of every soul around me, both on the street and inside the buildings. Looking around I saw faces at windows and doors and wondered with terror how far this demonic infection had spread. "For when it blows on you," the voices continued, "it will steal away your soul..."

My nerve snapped. I ran through the crowds, pushing them aside as they laughed at my fear. I ran into the road, hoping that fortune would provide me with an empty cab and a way out of there. I spied a possible saviour and ran directly into his path.

"Watch it!" the young fellow shouted, pulling his horse under control. "You'll end up beneath the wheels."

"Thank you!" I replied, rather nonsensically in hindsight. I was simply joyful to hear an autonomous voice after that devilish chorus. I pulled myself into the cab and begged him to take me home.

"A harrowing encounter indeed," Holmes said, sitting up and swinging his legs off the chaise. "And yet, I am still forced to wonder why it is that you have come here?"

"I had thought that, given your name was included amongst the three, you would wish to be warned of the fact," Silence responded.

"Warned?" Holmes shrugged. "Of what? You offer no particular threat beyond attracting the attention of the masses, something I'm afraid I'm already only too familiar with thanks to my friend Watson and his rather prolific pen."

"You have drawn the attention of more than your reading public," Silence said, "if your name is on the lips of demons."

"But you see, Doctor, I do not believe in demons."

"Sadly, Holmes," Silence replied, "they believe in you."

He got to his feet. "I mean to look into this matter further, with or without your assistance. You have my card should you wish to talk further."

"Or indeed have the housekeeper exorcised."

For the first time, Dr Silence lost his calm, slamming the ferrule of his cane against the floorboards. "You joke, Holmes, it does not suit you! I respect the skill you possess in your chosen subject, it would be a courtesy for you to do the same of mine. This is a dark business and, whether you like it or not, it concerns you."

"Time will tell, Doctor," Holmes replied. "In the meanwhile, I thank you for your concern." He walked over to his chemical table and set to work mixing a solution. Clearly Dr Silence's audience was at an end.

I got to my feet and, somewhat awkwardly, shook our guest's hand and escorted him to the front door.

On my return, Holmes was busying himself with the bubble of chemicals and the hiss of the Bunsen burner.

"That was ill-mannered, Holmes," I said, "even for you."

Holmes shrugged. "What do I care for manners? They are simply an affectation that hides the truth. Manners are no friend to the detective."

I picked up the morning paper and left him to his investigations; when he was in such a surly mood there was nothing to be gained from talking to him.

However, a few minutes later I was forced to break the silence. "Holmes?" I asked. "What were the three names mentioned by Silence?"

Holmes did not look up from his work as he replied: "Hilary De Montfort, the Laird of Boleskine and my good self. Why, have you had a premonition of your own, my friend?"

"Rather more than that," I replied, turning the paper towards him and quoting one of the articles. "'Young socialite found dead in baffling circumstances.'" I tossed the paper to him and he glanced at it while stirring a light-pink mixture that was frothing within the grip of the retort stand.

"Hilary De Montfort, son of the esteemed Lord Gabriel De Montfort, was found dead this morning in Grosvenor Square. The police remain tight-lipped about the circumstances but eyewitness reports suggest the body was found in..." Holmes raised a single eyebrow, "an extremely alarming state." He flung the newspaper back to me. "Save me from the language of the press, it pretends to say so much and yet offers nothing in the way of *facts*."

"Perhaps we may find those in the notebook of Inspector Gregson?" I suggested. "Had you read the article further you would see that he is in charge of the case."

"Gregson?" Holmes gave an appreciative smile. His feelings towards the inspector were as favourable as towards any man of that profession, in fact he had once gone as far as to refer to him as "the smartest of the Scotland Yarders". "Then maybe it is worth the cab fare after all." He gave a dry chuckle.

"What do you think it means?" I asked. "That this young man's name should have been mentioned by Silence...?"

"It means that the esteemed doctor wishes to secure my curiosity." Holmes turned off his Bunsen burner, peering at the simmering mixture he had created before getting to his feet and retrieving his jacket. "In which," he continued, "he has very much succeeded."

CHAPTER FOUR

THE BEST OF THE SCOTLAND YARDERS

We took a cab to Scotland Yard where Gregson was happy as always to receive us.

"It distracts me from the paperwork, gentlemen," he said, gesturing towards the various notes and forms that adorned his desk, "and in truth the affair is such a bizarre one I would appreciate any input you may have. I certainly don't know what to make of it."

He proceeded to describe the details of De Montfort's last hours, while I made notes and Holmes listened intently.

"Bizarre indeed," Holmes agreed, "and the second inexplicable thing I have heard today." He offered me a quick smile. "But then, as Watson will insist on telling his readers, explaining the inexplicable has become something of a theme. I don't suppose we might be allowed to see the body?"

Gregson scratched at his moustache. "Highly irregular of course, but I can't see there's anyone who'd object, seeing as it's you."

"Excellent!" Holmes declared.

I was only to glad to leave Scotland Yard. To me, with its raucous mixture of criminals being processed and officers trying to keep the peace, it has always felt like a factory floor. A foundry for crime perhaps. For certainly, only the most naïve of citizens could look on the long rows of unfortunates queued before the duty officer or scuffling together in the holding cells and think they were looking at the rehabilitated. For many of London's criminals, the time spent in the police stations and gaols of the capital were simply brief respites on the long road of their criminal career.

Holmes, Gregson and I made the short journey to the Metropolitan Morgue, a dismal edifice of soot-stained brick and dirty tile. Like many of the city's poorer hospitals, the stench when one crossed the threshold was of disinfectant combined with old blood and rotting flesh, the living attempting to eradicate the dead. While I had no doubt that the morgue officers made every effort to keep a clean laboratory, there was only so much you could do when your drawers were forever filling with the cadavers of yet more unfortunates. There were the bloated bodies of those fished from the Thames, and the half-rotted (and often half-eaten) remains of those dumped in the darker corners of our city or the tunnels underneath it. When I am in one of my darker moods – what Holmes would describe as a "brown study" – I often think we live in a city built on the bones of the dead.

"Welcome, gentlemen," Cuthbert Wells said, a police surgeon of our acquaintance, "what brings you back amongst the ranks of the brutally deceased?"

"We wish to examine what remains of Hilary De Montfort," Holmes responded.

"Then you are only just in time," Wells replied, "his family are impatient to claim him for their own." He smiled. "There is snobbery even beyond the mortal coil," he explained, "and they do not like the company their son has fallen into."

Holmes glanced around at the cold halls. "I am not sure I blame them."

"Come now, Holmes," laughed Wells, "you have dabbled in less salubrious quarters, I'm sure."

"If we could see the body, then?" Gregson interrupted, impatient to be at the business in hand.

"But of course, gentlemen," Wells replied. "Follow me."

He led us through to one of the small dissecting rooms. The body of young De Montfort was laid out on the slab beneath its heavy sheet.

Holmes whipped the cloth back so as to fully appreciate the state of the corpse beneath. Even my famously cool friend couldn't quite hide his surprise at how battered the body was, drawing a quick breath between clenched teeth.

"The poor fellow is in a bad way. Watson, your opinion?"

I took his place at the dead body's side and, as was always the way once about the business of my profession, all emotional response to the man before me vanished, to be replaced by the cold, automatic response of the pathologist. I like to think that I am not a man who is without a sense of empathy – indeed according to Holmes it is something I possess to the point of distraction – but once reduced to a biological puzzle on the mortician's table, a body becomes just that. You are a thing of ligature marks and contusions, a book to be read from. I have never caught a glimpse of the human soul in an empty cadaver.

"If I didn't know better," I said, "I would suggest he died from a considerable fall. The last time I saw such wounds was when my wife and I went hiking in Wales." I looked up towards my fellows.

"Something of a marred holiday as Mary and I stumbled on a young man who had fallen from the Blorenge."

"We wondered if he was the victim of several assailants," commented Gregson, "if a handful of men gave him a sound kicking..."

"...Then the wounds would have been quite different," explained Wells. "The majority of the damage is caused by one, relatively even, blow."

"Such as one would expect had a man fallen from a great height," I agreed, "or perhaps had something dropped upon him."

"Then you would expect a more even crushing of the bones," Wells said, "whereas the damage here is shallow yet dramatic." He clapped his hands together. "The bones are shattered, the bruising prodigious."

"Which doesn't make any sense," Gregson said.

"The inexplicable it is then," Holmes said.

We left the mortuary bound for Grosvenor Square. Holmes gazing out of the cab window and refusing to enter into our discussions as we moved through the city streets. He had thoughts of his own and had never been one to suppress them for the sake of public chat.

"I fear this is going to be a mystery that remains so," Gregson said. "An investigator needs some fuel to fire him and this affair exists in a vacuum."

"Surely you must have been close to the truth when you suggested he was attacked by a gang of roughs," I said. "A base crime of opportunity, ruffians eager for what he may have carried in his purse?"

"It was my first thought, for we could not locate his purse," Gregson admitted, "but murderers like that don't chase their quarry through the streets, they leap out of a dark corner, strike quickly, then fade away."

I thought about it for a moment. "Unless one of the attackers was known to De Montfort?" I suggested. "Perhaps a member of staff at one of the clubs? Working with a gang, tipping them off as to who would make rich pickings on their way home? If that were the case they could hardly allow him to escape. Say they attacked him but he broke free – hence he was seen running through the streets by your eyewitness – but they ran him to ground in Grosvenor Square, determined to silence him in case he informed the police of their involvement."

"It's a workable hypothesis, Doctor," the inspector agreed, "and one that had occurred to me."

Of course it had, I thought, amused at the fact that Gregson couldn't bear to allow another to appear to have one up on him.

I looked to Holmes for some small sign of corroboration but he was still in the depths of his own thoughts, watching the buildings fly by beyond the cab window.

Once we arrived at the square, Holmes was quick to snap out of his daze, hopping down from the cab and dashing off into the snow.

"I'm afraid there will be little to see, Mr Holmes," Gregson said, following at a distance.

"Certainly any useful story the ground may have chosen to tell has all but been erased," Holmes agreed. "But it's valuable to get a sense of the place."

He looked around, pointing his cane before him like the needle of a compass as he surveyed the park and pictured the night before. "De Montfort enters from the north via Brook Street," he said, "running towards the centre." He followed in what must have been the young man's footsteps. "Why, I wonder?"

"Presumably he was trying to shake his pursuers," I said.

"If you were being chased through the streets by a gang of ruffians, Watson," my friend replied, "then surely you would stick to the main thoroughfare? All the while shouting for assistance?"

"I suppose you would," I admitted.

"So he entered the park for a reason," Holmes insisted. "One that he felt might save his life."

"Can we really look for logic in the man's last panicked movements?" asked Gregson. "Surely he was simply running scared?"

"No," Holmes replied, "his flight wasn't random. According to your evidence he was walking from Knaves on St James's Street to Salieri's on Brook Street. If he was simply running in fear he would hardly have gone so far out of his way. He came here for a reason."

"Which was?" the inspector asked, not without a degree of irritation.

"If I knew that, Gregson," Holmes replied, "I would hardly still be stood here."

He gave Gregson a brief smile and then began to stride towards the south exit. "Come, Watson," he shouted, "time to consult an expert."

CHAPTER FIVE

AN EXPERT IN TITTLE-TATTLE

Holmes and I left Gregson and headed towards Berkeley Square.

"I fear you've put our poor colleague in a bad mood," I said with a smile.

"Colleague?" replied Holmes. "You flatter him."

We continued our stroll through London's more affluent areas, retracing the last journey of Hilary De Montfort as we worked our way to St James's Street and its illustrious rows of private clubs.

"This expert you wish to consult, Holmes," I said. "Would I be correct in assuming it to be Langdale Pike?"

"Indeed, Watson," my friend replied, "there is no better man in London for shining a light on the movements of its social circle. If we wish to achieve an insight into Mr De Montfort, Pike is the man to help us."

I couldn't disagree with Holmes, though he knows only too well that I have no great love for Langdale Pike.

Pike had been a college friend of Holmes and had also risen to the top of an unusual profession. That profession, however, was one I found it hard to approve of. Pike was a gossipmonger, a trader in secrets and scandals. A number of the less respectable newspapers carried his columns, and London's glittering socialites – vain moths who believed themselves to be butterflies – fluttered around him, despite the frequent harshness of his tongue. In the world of the socialite, there was only one thing worse than being talked about and that, as Oscar Wilde so astutely said, was *not* being talked about. In the rarefied atmosphere of the theatre openings and galas, the house parties and regattas, gossips like Pike were the fuel that kept your star burning brightly.

His "office" was the bowed window of his club on St James's Street where he would sit, a small notebook close to hand which he would consult or add to as the day went on. He was a receiving house, a bottomless pit of flimsy news and allegation, topped up by every servant's whisper or jilted lover's accusation. From his pocket he would pull sharp, clean banknotes, paying out for every nugget of worth. And he paid well, he could afford to. Rumour had it that he earned a four-figure sum per annum from his newspaper articles. Which, as someone who has some experience in publishing, is no mean task I can assure you.

Holmes was tolerant of Pike's occupation – indeed he often traded information with him – but personally I considered him to represent everything I found reprehensible about modern society.

Upon spotting us through the window Pike smiled and gave a delicate, regal wave.

We were led through to his private lounge by an elderly waiter who gazed upon the perpetually flamboyant Pike as if caught in the glare of the silk lining of his jacket.

"My dear Sherlock!" Pike rose and clasped Holmes' hand. There was a sweet puff of cologne as Pike opened his arms and gestured for

us to sit. "You will of course join me for lunch? There is some quite
exquisite game pie." For once, my natural inclination towards dining
was tempered. I had no great desire to eat in this man's company.
Perversely, Holmes, a man whose main subsistence was tobacco,
informed Pike that we would do so with pleasure.

"To what do I owe this visit, Sherlock?" Pike asked. "Or can I
guess?"

"I would be disappointed if you couldn't," Holmes admitted.

Pike chuckled. "You have come to find out what I know of the late
Hilary De Montfort," he said, "in the hope that I can shed some light
on what is unquestionably one of the most bizarre deaths to have
reached my ears in the last twenty-four hours."

"Not longer?" I asked, somewhat sarcastically.

"My dear Doctor," Pike replied, "this is London, where the bizarre
is a daily occurrence, thank God. If it were not so then I imagine both
Sherlock and I would be forced to relocate."

"I fear you give the city too much credit," said Holmes, "it has been
many weeks since something has threatened to grasp my attention."

"Ah, but then you always were hard to please, I find the streets
positively bristling with intrigue."

"It takes more than *affaires* and new frocks to stimulate me,"
Holmes agreed. "I am also fiercely impatient."

Pike sighed and reached for his little notebook. "Indeed you are."
He shuffled through the pages, apparently refreshing his memory. I
doubt Holmes was fooled. Given De Montfort's very recent demise
there was little doubt in my mind that Pike had already reminded
himself of all he knew in preparation for writing about it.

"Of course," he said finally, "young Hilary was always the black
sheep of the De Montfort family. But then with such a boring clan

that's not difficult. Old money, old land. The sort of family that place more stock on knowing family history than they do current affairs. Heads in the past."

"A family of noble heritage in other words," I countered.

Pike shrugged. "If you say so. I see nothing worthwhile in looking in any other direction but towards the future."

"Whereas, presumably," Holmes said, "young Hilary struggled to look beyond the here and now?"

"One would imagine so," Pike said, "though Hilary's interests were considerably broader than you might imagine. In fact he was a member of the Golden Dawn."

"The Golden Dawn?" I asked, "What's that? One of the new gentlemen's clubs?"

"Not quite," Pike said. "The Hermetic Order of the Golden Dawn is an occult society, Doctor, which counts a number of celebrities amongst its ranks. The actress Florence Farr among them."

"Well," I said, "there's no telling what she gets up to."

"Indeed," Pike agreed. "I'm afraid there's no telling what any of them get up to. I know relatively little about what goes on there."

Holmes raised a surprised eyebrow.

"They wouldn't let me join," Pike explained, causing Holmes to bark a laugh and clap his hands.

"By what standards were you unsuitable?" he asked.

"I think they could tell that my intent was not as honourable as it might be. In truth I have no great knowledge or belief in magic beyond what I see on the London stage."

"It is a serious group then?" I asked.

"Deadly so," Pike replied. "It sprang from the membership of the Freemasons as a society to promote the practice of occult rituals and what they termed 'spiritual development'. I imagine it has a great deal to do with slitting the throats of livestock and wearing appalling robes."

"So what draws a man like Hilary De Montfort to join their ranks?" Holmes asked.

"Aside from the loose morals of the members?" Pike responded with a raised eyebrow.

"I imagine," I suggested, "that, like the Freemasons, there's a good deal of mutual backscratching. Perhaps he sought to improve his social standing?"

"His social standing was hardly lacking," Pike scoffed. "He was a pretty young fellow with money to burn, such people are unassailable in society."

"Perhaps it was the excitement?" Holmes said. "The lure of the illicit."

"Now that's more likely," Pike agreed. "Hilary was a man who bored easily."

"Then he has my sympathies," Holmes said, as the old man entered with our food.

Pike's epicurean tastes were as well honed as one might imagine. The game pie was indeed excellent, even if the lunch conversation challenged my digestion.

"What's your opinion as to the manner of his death?" Holmes asked Pike.

"Surely he was set upon by a gang," Pike replied. "From what I hear of the state of his body, there can be little other explanation."

"But it's simply not possible," I said. Despite having said something similar to Gregson myself, I found, the more that I considered the dead body, the less I could believe it. "The wounds just don't conform with such a hypothesis. I'd stake my profession on it."

"You are lucky that you don't have to," replied Holmes. "Given the inexplicable nature of the crime and the importance of the victim's family, considerable pressure will no doubt be put on Wells, the police surgeon, to endorse such a palatable opinion."

"They will want the matter dealt with swiftly, certainly," Pike agreed. "For families of that pedigree, truth is not as important as appearance. It is an embarrassment that must be made to go away."

"No matter the cost?" I asked.

"The cost is ours to spare, noble Watson," Holmes said with a smile, "as long as we can explain the inexplicable. Again."

He turned to Pike. "Tell me Langdale, what is your opinion of Dr John Silence?"

"Ah!" Pike's face lit up even brighter. "The medical scourge of the netherworld? I think he's probably a gentle, well-meaning lunatic."

"Then you and Holmes are in agreement," I said.

"No, Watson," Holmes said, "I have by no means decided whether he means well. One final question," he said to Pike, brushing the crumbs of the game pie from his lips with his napkin, "before I am so indebted to you that it takes me years to balance the books by providing you with tittle-tattle."

"My dear Sherlock," Pike said, "I've told you nothing, you cleared your debt simply by consenting to be my lunch companions. What is this final question of yours?"

"The Laird of Boleskine," Holmes said. "Is the title familiar to you?"

Pike laughed. "Indeed it is, though you've come to the right man for certainly you won't find mention of it in any gazetteer. The Laird of Boleskine is self-proclaimed and far from an official position. It is the name young Aleister Crowley has given himself since buying his new house in Scotland."

"Aleister Crowley?" I asked, entirely unfamiliar with the name.

"A writer and mountaineer," Pike replied, "and a man fast earning himself the title of the 'wickedest man in the world.'"

CHAPTER SIX

INTERLUDE: THE PECULIAR SUPPER OF LORD RUTHVNEY

Lord Bartholomew Ruthvney helped himself to a cigar and topped up his glass of brandy. The fire cracked like a coachman's whip in its grate and added wisps of dark smoke to the room. Ruthvney tutted – he would remonstrate with the housekeeper in the morning, a well-cleaned chimney should not smoke. He stood away, marching proudly across a bearskin rug towards the far wall where his display cases stood.

Ruthvney enjoyed many hobbies. He was a man of keen appetite (as any who had joined him at the dinner table could attest) but nothing gave him greater pleasure than hunting. The pursuit and capture of another living creature, to Ruthvney, was an act so powerful that it left him lightheaded. It was, he believed, as close as a man might come to God. He puffed mouthfuls of cigar smoke against the glass that encased his exhibits as he strolled amongst them, remembering each pull of the trigger. He looked into cold, glass eyes and imagined their last spark of life. If only it could be captured along with the animal's pelts. How much more precious that would be, a cabinet of fragile, flickering light, each held frozen at the point of extinction.

There was a knock at the door. Stevens, Ruthvney's butler, entered. "Is there anything else I can do for you, sir?" he asked.

"Not unless you have a sweep hidden away in the wine cellar," Ruthvney replied. "That useless woman Pritchard has allowed the chimney to become congested, the damned thing is coughing smoke into the room."

"My apologies, sir," Stevens replied. "I will of course insist the situation is remedied."

"See that you do," replied Ruthvney. "I have no wish to choke to death in my own study."

Stevens gave a small bow and retired. Ruthvney returned to admiring his collection.

As well as the usual mounted heads, Ruthvney had begun to collect other stuffed creatures. Coiled serpents, bears reeling, foxes with fangs bared. His collection was a perfect snapshot of death and he loved every bit of it.

Behind him the coals crumpled in the grate, sending out a plume of sparks. He watched the sparks fade as they cooled on the wooden floor, making no move to extinguish them and preserve his floorboards. Such mundane care taking was not for the likes of him, he would have considered it a breakdown in social protocol to even consider it. Let the wood be scorched – his eyes were raised to higher duties.

Which reminded him of that morning's correspondence, as yet untouched. He sat at his desk, placing his cigar on the rim of a heavy, cut-glass ashtray that glinted on the green leather.

He kept his filing simple, placing everything worthy of his attention in the top, left-hand drawer until he had dealt with it, at which point

he would move it to the right (or, more often still, into the fire grate – Ruthvney was not a sentimental man and saw no point in keeping his letters unless they contained information of importance).

He pulled out a small pile of letters and placed them on the desk in front of him, taking a moment to draw on his cigar as he reached for his brass letter opener.

The first was a request for money from a charitable organisation. It was discarded, barely read, for the fire.

The second was a request for further tunnelling work on the underground railway. Ruthvney was in the financially embarrassing position of being one of the Central London Railway's major shareholders. In truth he rued the day he had ever become involved, at the way the business was currently running he may as well have ploughed his money directly into the dirt beneath the city. Certainly that is what he had done in spirit. They said it would open soon... after only ten years of planning and work! He tossed the letter to one side where it could stop vexing his digestion.

The third was yet another call on his bank account. He was on the Board of Governors for the Lidster School for Girls, a dowdy establishment languishing somewhere in the north. It would seem their gymnasium was in need of repair, for which he was expected to share the bill. The headmistress, a creature of lace and cobwebs known as Mrs Shuttle (if she had ever had a Christian name it was long lost through her years of dispensing education), said it was "important for the future health of our charges". Ruthvney added it to charity letter.

Next came an invitation to attend the theatrical opening of a new play. Ruthvney did not like the theatre. The theatre was loud and full of expectation. One was expected to laugh in all the right places, cry in all the right places... Ruthvney did not enjoy labouring under such pressure. It joined the pile of kindling.

The fire cracked again, a loud rifle shot that momentarily put him in mind of the safari plains. He coughed, the smoke irritating his throat. He took a large mouthful of brandy, hoping it would help, and returned to his letters.

Next was a summons to a dinner party, an evening of old war stories and fatty pheasant with Major Thorkipps and his gluttonous wife. He'd probably go, the hosts were a terrible bore but for reasons he could never quite fathom they were well thought of in society and often attracted interesting additions to their dining table.

Finally, a small, black envelope that, once opened, revealed little more than a thick piece of vellum with a line of strange symbols upon it.

Ruthvney held it up to the light and examined the writing. What the devil was it?

There was a roar of wind from outside the French windows and Ruthvney dropped the piece of paper, startled, despite himself. Shaken from his confusion, he picked up the scrap of paper, placed it on the pile of letters for burning and got to his feet.

The wind roared again, the French windows swelling in their frame with a loud creak.

Storm coming, Ruthvney thought, probably keep him awake for most of the night.

The wind blew once more and this time it was so strong he thought it would push the doors wide open.

He got to his feet, holding onto the edge of the desk as his head fizzed with dizziness. Probably the smoke, he thought, taking another mouthful of brandy, draining the glass. Like a badger in its set, I'm being smoked out.

He moved over to the French windows, wanting to ensure they were locked tight and draw the curtains to keep as much of the foul night at bay as he could.

The doors were, indeed, locked. He looked out on the moonlit grounds, the hems of the curtains in his hands. The moon was bright, he noticed, so maybe there wouldn't be a storm after all. The trees were lashing back and forth almost fit to uproot themselves though, so who could tell what clouds would be blown over later?

He yanked the curtains closed. Then immediately drew them back again, sure he had glimpsed something just before the heavy fabric had obscured his view. Yes! Out there on the far edge of the lawn, three figures, walking slowly towards the house. What the deuce time was this for callers? Too late for legitimate business, he thought, watching as they pushed their way against the wind, forcing themselves step by slow step closer to the building. Too late by half. He'd give them a welcome!

He moved back into his study aiming for where his rifle was kept in the case beyond his desk. Suddenly his head grew dizzy again, a moment of terrible nausea as his entire body swayed. It was as if he were on the deck of a ship, nothing steady, nothing still. He put a hand out against the wall, trying to recover himself. Was it the smoke? he wondered. Could it disorientate a man so much? There was a low growl from behind him and he turned to see the stuffed bear straining its dust-filled limbs. Then a rattle as the dead snake twitched the dry bones in its tail. What was this?

Ruthvney staggered across the room, his hands flailing ahead of him as they reached for the gun cabinet. The fire roared. The smoke continued to trickle past the mantel and creep up the wall, leaving thin, sooty trails in its wake.

Ruthvney tugged the keys to the cabinet from his waistcoat ticket pocket where they hung from his watch chain. He unlocked the cabinet, removed the rifle and turned to face the far end of the room where his taxidermy was now quite still. What on earth was he thinking? Of course it was still, there was no life left in that menagerie.

But there was still the matter of the strangers outside, the three men making their way towards the house. Unless they too had been a delusion?

No! Ruthvney wouldn't have it... He was not a man who imagined things, he was a man of facts, of solid truths. He walked back towards the French windows, rifle in hand, but made it only halfway across the room before a pain in his stomach doubled him over.

What was happening to him? First he began seeing things then this... this... what? The pain was not like the indigestion that frequently troubled him, nor was it the equally familiar stab of trapped wind. No, this was something that he had experienced often enough but so powerful, so savagely heightened, that it took him a moment to recognise it. The pain was *hunger*. An aching, desperate need to fill his stomach.

This was not the time! He forced his way on, determined to see off the strangers he had seen. He managed a few more feet before the pain struck him again, savage, undeniable...

He stepped back a few paces, resting against his desk as his stomach churned and begged for food. He turned, barking short yaps of pain as he grabbed at anything that might quell this aching pain in his guts. He tore at the desk blotter, the rifle falling from his hands as he shoved chunks of thick paper into his mouth. For a brief moment the pain seemed to dip, softening as he felt the lumps of paper pass along his throat. Then it returned, just as pronounced as before, perhaps more so. He needed more, something of more substance...

He looked around the room, tugging his cravat from his throat as he searched for something to satisfy him. He wedged the thin silk into a solid ball, popped it into his mouth and swallowed it. Again, that momentary relief only for the need to return even more pronounced.

His eyes passed over the French windows, all thought of the strangers outside gone. All he felt was hunger.

He ran to the far end of the room, moving among his display cases. These creatures would sustain him, he realised. They may no longer have the meat they once did, but there was still skin to be had, thick leather and cured pelt. He reached for the head of a young elk but the hooks held it fast and he was forced to stretch up on tiptoe, chewing at its dry snout, pulling off short strips of skin with his teeth, chewing and tearing more, his wet lips coated in dust.

More! More!

He turned to the display cabinets, smashing the glass with his fists and grabbing the heartiest specimens he could. He held the fox in his arms, chewing on its ear, raking its flanks with his nails desperate to pull some the skin loose.

His teeth chipped and dislodged in his gums, not built for such sturdy work.

Finally, he got the meat he craved, though the relief was short-lived as he choked violently on his own tongue.

Breathless and delirious he fell to the floor, gazing purple-faced at the ceiling, his tongue lodging firmly at the back of his throat, wedged there alongside a dusty chunk of sawdust and bone.

At the periphery of his vision he was just aware of the wind crashing into his study, the French windows forced open.

The three figures stepped in, one moved towards his desk, another towards the fire.

Ruthvney died and they went about their business.

CHAPTER SEVEN

THE RETURN OF SILENCE

The story of Lord Ruthvney's death coincided with my breakfast as I perused the morning edition at the dining table. I would like to say that it affected my appetite but that would be a lie. I'm an ex-soldier, once you've sipped soup under cannon fire there's little that can interfere with your digestion.

"Have you seen this, Holmes?" I asked as my friend strolled in from his bedroom, his un-oiled hair hanging over his eyes like a curtain. "It strikes me as *recherché* enough for your attention." I folded the paper so as to give the article due prominence and tossed it next to his breakfast plate, then helped myself to another kipper.

"Ah." Holmes sighed. "Such is my lot: to become an investigator of the odd, a policeman of clowns." He glanced at the article and raised an eyebrow. "Though certainly it is hard to ignore such a death as this." He gave the article his full attention for a few moments, then tossed it aside. "Well," he said, lifting the lid on the dish of eggs,

"Lord Ruthvney clearly died a madman's death. The question must be whether his lack of sanity was a new condition or one brought about by the involvement of others." He scooped a couple of eggs onto his plate. "Either way. It is no business of ours, we have more than enough to occupy us."

"Have you come to any conclusions?"

"Only that the good Dr Silence is clearly determined to gain our attention in this matter."

"Well, yes, he would hardly have sought an appointment otherwise."

"But why?" Holmes asked. "What is it for? He has neither engaged our services or set us a mystery to solve."

"The death of De Montfort."

"Is part of the whole story, certainly. But how big a part?" He began to eat his eggs.

"What makes you think the young man's murder is so incidental?"

"One simply doesn't go to so much effort to murder a social butterfly like De Montfort. If somebody wanted him dead then a drop of poison in an overpriced glass of champagne would serve the purpose perfectly well. His death was a piece of theatre, designed to cause attention, murderers who do that are rarely singular in their focus for victims."

"Why draw attention to murder?" I wondered aloud. There were several possibilities of course: a distraction, perhaps, or a warning. I said as much to Holmes.

"Indeed," he agreed, "or a message of some kind."

"A grisly telegram if so."

Holmes threw up his hands in despair. "There simply isn't enough evidence upon which to theorise." He got to his feet and paced, irritated, amongst the usual piles of detritus with which he littered the floor of our rooms: newspapers, police reports, charcoal sketches... It was as if Holmes' brain leaked. He stopped at the window and turned back to me, all trace of despondency now gone. "But here is more coal for our engine, Watson!" he shouted. "The enigmatic Dr Silence has returned!"

He resumed his place at the breakfast table and attacked the toast rack with the vigour of a man starved. When Dr Silence was ushered into our rooms by Mrs Hudson it was to be presented to a man who gave the impression his life depended on the greater consumption of marmalade.

"Sit down, Doctor," Holmes said. "Take some coffee and toast. Mrs Hudson has as much an idea of breakfast as any Scotswoman and I'm sure she will be happy to accommodate one more."

Mrs Hudson sighed. "Of course she will," she said. "Given the other things I accommodate in his household, an extra mouth is nothing."

"I'll take the coffee gladly," said our guest, "but I've already breakfasted."

Holmes shrugged and resumed his spooning of marmalade onto toast. "To what do we owe the repeated pleasure of your company, Dr Silence?" he asked.

"You have seen the morning editions I see," Silence said, gesturing towards my discarded newspaper, "and have no doubt read of the peculiar death of Lord Ruthvney?"

Holmes paused momentarily, toast held halfway between plate and mouth. "Indeed," he said. "In fact, we were just discussing it."

"What you probably do not know is that he was, like young De Montfort, a member of the Golden Dawn."

"Like De Montfort and the Laird of Boleskine himself, Mr Aleister Crowley," added Holmes, watching intently for Silence's response.

The man gave very little, simply nodded and continued to speak.

"You have investigated along similar lines to myself, I see," he said, "though it would seem Mr Crowley is no longer affiliated with the organisation."

"You've spoken to him?"

"No, I believe he rarely leaves Boleskine House these days, though certainly I think we should."

"'We?'" Holmes asked with a slight smile.

"I had thought that considering the news you might cease your feigned disinterest and help with the investigation."

I drew a short breath at Dr Silence's choice of words – Holmes did not like to "help" anyone with an investigation, not the official force and most certainly not someone he deemed, at best, deluded. Holmes wasted no time in correcting him.

"I am not what one might call a 'team player', Doctor. If indeed I choose to investigate the matter, you can rest assured I will be doing so entirely of my own volition and not in partnership with someone else."

"Would it damage your ego to occasionally share notes?" Silence asked. "Possibly even a rail carriage? Given that we will be following the same trail it seems churlish to ignore each other en route. Besides, you scarcely begin to know what we're dealing with. I have not been idle these last couple of days and have much to pass on."

Holmes laughed. "My dear Doctor, you must forgive my professional vanity. Perhaps you are right, we should work in tandem. After all, it is a world of which I know precious little. Pray, tell me your news."

"I thought the promise of more information might loosen your manner." Silence smiled. "I dare say you have not been idle either and will soon be able to inform me of developments from your end?"

Homes said nothing but inclined his head in acceptance.

"I have been researching this so-called Breath of God. It is a phenomena frequently mentioned in the biblical apocrypha as well as other, less wholesome, texts. In some scriptures it is said that the Breath of God was the method of destruction for the twin cities of Sodom and Gomorrah, God's angels acting as a conduit for his 'almighty essence'. Some also suggest that Moses called down the Breath of God to destroy those Israelites who chose not to follow the Ten Commandments. Some scholars insist it is intended to be synonymous with God's power, a poetic phrase intended to liven up the scripture. Others contend that it is literally what it suggests: a fearsome, elemental force capable of mass destruction. Capable even of killing a man in the open air, leaving no other sign of attack."

"It's something of a jump to assume De Montfort was slaughtered by divine halitosis simply because we currently flounder to find more conventional answers," insisted Holmes. "You'll forgive me if I pursue more earthly means for now?"

"I would expect little else," Silence replied, "and no doubt you will be more interested to hear that my sources claim there is dissent amongst the ranks of the Golden Dawn. Dissent that saw De Montfort, Ruthvney and Crowley in agreement against those more senior than themselves within the organisation. Is that an earthly enough reason to suspect Crowley of being the next victim?"

Holmes considered. "It's enough to make me dip my hand in my pocket for a rail fare, certainly. Watson, check the Bradshaw for trains to Inverness. Allow me the morning, however. As first we must ask our accommodating friends at Scotland Yard to allow us access to yet another murder room."

CHAPTER EIGHT

RUTHVNEY HALL

The estate of the recently deceased Lord Ruthvney was located just north of Billericay en route to Chelmsford. Agreeing to meet Silence at St Pancras for the four o'clock to Inverness, Holmes and I made our way first to Scotland Yard, then Liverpool Street and, thenceforth, for the country.

Despite my love for London I do enjoy visiting the open country; the air is revitalising, the scenery enriching. Holmes did not feel the same. In fact, for most of the time I knew him, he acted as if the open air was sheer poison to him, like a sea creature pulled from his familiar rock pool and forced to wither in the sunshine. I have seen him nearly choke to death when placed on a hill in a strong breeze. It is an argument for evolution certainly, that a man so immersed in smoke and fog now needs it to survive. Of course, he would later retire to the country which proves what a contrary swine he could often be.

"The chief investigating officer is a local," Holmes said, "an Inspector

Mann. A good fellow by all accounts who is only too happy to tolerate our presence."

It would be thought that any police officer would welcome assistance from someone as famously insightful and – perhaps more importantly – happy to pass on the credit as Holmes. Experience had frequently taught us otherwise. Holmes is of the opinion that there will come a time when the consulting detective is so common in society that he will no longer bear the jibes of the official forces, rather such a proliferation will in itself bring about a change in how crime is detected. He foresees a time when deduction is compartmentalised, a nation of experts of every possible stripe. You wish to investigate a poisoning? Then you would call on the consultant who specialises in deadly venoms. Someone has been shot? Then you would talk to a detective who specialises in gun crime. Personally I wasn't convinced the police force would devolve in this manner. Experience showed that Holmes' methods were initially distrusted, sometimes outright loathed. Once he had built a working relationship with the officer in question things might be different – there were a number of young officers rising through the force thanks in no small part to the patronage of Holmes – but on first meeting I could recall none that had warmed to him. Even less so once he had mocked their methods and then proceeded to apply his own.

However, in the case of Inspector George Mann I was to find an exception to this rule. From the first he was graciousness itself and it was clear that he hoped to learn as much from Holmes as their time together would allow. Such an attitude stood him in excellent stead with my friend of course, a man who has never found a compliment he didn't like. Mann was in his early thirties and sported a beard so neatly trimmed one could tell one was in the company of a fastidious man. His waistline, while far from the excesses of, say, Holmes' brother Mycroft, also suggested a man who enjoyed the sensual pleasures in life. It was the belly of a man who shared my opinion that, as important as deduction might be, it shouldn't be allowed to get in the way of meal times.

Having greeted us at the local station, Mann had provided a trap so that we might easily get to Lord Ruthvney's estate. While we traversed the quaint, narrow roads, he did his best to fill us in on the investigation thus far.

"To be honest," he admitted, "it's not the sort of business we're used to handling. It seems from the outside of it to be a case of suicide, albeit it by a method we can't claim to have seen before."

"The newspapers say he died from ingesting 'foreign matter'," I said. "Can you be a little more specific?"

"He consumed a heroic quantity of his own taxidermy collection," said Mann, "causing considerable damage to his teeth and jaw as he did so."

"Had he exhibited previous signs of being mentally unstable?" I asked.

"Not in the least," said Mann. "In fact he was the very model of rural respectability."

"Bar his occult hobby at least," commented Holmes, "though maybe that is more de rigeur outside London."

"Occult?" Mann asked.

"He was a member of the occult society the Hermetic Order of the Golden Dawn," I explained. "A fact that we expect to have some bearing on the case."

Mann raised an eyebrow. "Really? I find that somewhat hard to believe."

"That he was a member or that it will have a bearing?" asked Holmes.

"Both frankly," Mann said. "Life is even more conservative amongst the rural gentry than in the cities, and Ruthvney was a regular face at the local church. In fact he had been known to take part in festivals, giving a reading at the Christmas mass and so on. You know what it's like with these people, they think it's important to play a fairly central role in local life."

"Indeed," Holmes agreed, "and perhaps it is that rather than any real devotion that saw him take part in local worship."

"Perhaps," Mann admitted.

"And yet you do not believe it?" Holmes said.

Mann smiled. "If you have it on good authority then it seems I'll have to," he replied.

We arrived at Ruthvney Hall, an austere pile of bricks that cast a gloomy shadow over its well-kept lawns.

The trap pulled up on the gravel of the entrance court and we all climbed out.

"What would you like to do first, Mr Holmes?" Mann asked. "Inspect the study or interview the staff?"

Holmes smiled. "Inspect the study I think, let the lay of the land inform before the opinions of the help distract."

We followed Mann to the room in question and he stepped back to allow Holmes access. Both myself and the inspector watched from the doorway as Holmes went about his usual investigation. Watching Holmes at work, I am often reminded of the descriptions of how Native Americans went about the tracking of animals. They read volumes in the depth of mere dust, in the angle of a paw print or the quantity of shed hair. For Holmes the drawing room or front lawn were the more likely sites of his hunt than the plains of Utah or the green fields of the Midwest. But he went about it with alacrity, throwing himself into the scene of the crime and studying it on the most intimate level of which his senses were capable. He plotted traffic on the hearth rug by inconsistencies in its pile, identified a brand of furniture polish by a single hearty sniff and could analyse the emotional state of the char by a brief analysis of the mantel.

It was an act that I never failed to enjoy watching. It seemed that Mann was also an eager spectator. He observed silently, not interrupting as many of his fellows frequently did, determined to promote their own observational abilities rather than take note of Holmes'. At one point he removed his notebook and jotted a few observations down. I smiled – Holmes had found himself an eager student.

"The room offers several points that prove there was more to Ruthvney's final hours than a fit of madness," Holmes announced. "The fire was smoking abnormally as is shown by the tarry deposits on the tiles around the grate. I would want to analyse the powder I've collected from them before committing myself, but the soot certainly contains more than the simple remains of an open fire, *something* abnormal was burned there."

"Something that could have caused Ruthvney's behaviour?" I asked.

"You're thinking of the *Radix pedis diaboli*?" my friend replied with a smile.

I confess I was. A recent case where the root of an African plant had been burned in a sealed room, the smoke it released causing madness and death to those who inhaled it.

"It could certainly have been something along those lines," Holmes admitted. "Something affected Ruthvney unfavourably enough for him to start dining on his collection." He poked delicately through the shattered glass with the toe of his boot. "And, given the bloodstains on this glass, numbed his pain sufficiently for him to pay his wounds scant attention."

"So it's a matter of poison then you believe, sir?" Mann asked.

Holmes held up his hand. "Please, Inspector, these are initial impressions. While further investigation may prove them to be facts, it would be a grievous mistake to treat them as such for now. Tell me, did you or your men take anything from this room?"

"No sir, I was particularly determined to avoid such a thing, I knew that you would wish to examine everything just as it was."

"Most kind, and it is immediately useful in that it confirms one thing for us: someone removed something from Ruthvney's desk after his death."

"How can you be so sure?" I asked.

"Because there are four letters and five envelopes," he said, sitting down at the desk. "He was clearly going through his correspondence just prior to his unfortunate attack. The desk is tidy, he is not a man who leaves his letters lying around. Here we have a pile of letters. An invitation to a play and one to a dinner party, a letter concerning his position as governor of a school, and a request for a charity donation. The latter, you will notice, opened first and destined for refusal, filed as it was beneath the five envelopes." Holmes looked around. "There is no basket for waste paper and yet he is a tidy man so presumably he intended to throw them in the fire. The fact he didn't do so means that he was interrupted. So where is the fifth letter and what was it?"

"Surely a man would go through his correspondence at the start of the day?" I asked.

"That rather depends whether the man in question cares to

respond. Lord Ruthvney clearly felt he could keep people waiting. He was also," Holmes gestured to the pile, "a man who received exceedingly boring post."

He lowered his face to the desk, and grinned. "There was also a sixth envelope!" he announced. "And presumably therefore a sixth letter." He looked to Mann. "He had nothing on him?"

"Not in the sense you mean, sir," Mann replied. "Certainly he had nothing which could have been posted to him."

Holmes removed his small leather tool pouch from his jacket pocket, untied it and removed a pair of tweezers. He picked up a small triangle of black paper from the surface of the desk. "A fragment of the envelope. You'll note he didn't use a letter opener – one often tears off the first piece of an envelope when one opens it by hand. Black paper, portentous as well as pretentious."

"Who writes using a black envelope?" I asked.

"Someone wishing to seem satanic!" Holmes dropped the paper fragment into a small envelope of its own, sealed it and placed it in his pocket. It then occurred to him that perhaps, as it was evidence, he should have offered it to Inspector Mann. "Oh," he said, somewhat awkwardly, "perhaps you should..."

The Inspector smiled. "Consider yourself a specialist drafted in under my authority. All I ask is that you share whatever you learn. I shall, of course, show you the same courtesy, though I suspect you will have more to tell me than I you."

Holmes clapped his hands and patted the envelope where it rested in his pocket. "I shall wring it dry of all it offers," he promised, "and send you my findings. He sat back at the desk, spreading out his hands on the soft green leather. He was, I knew, putting himself in the position of the now absent Ruthvney. "So," he said after a moment, "tell me what you have managed to glean with regard to the chain of events."

Mann smiled and flipped open his notebook, clearly he had been awaiting this cue. "According to Stevens, the butler, his master was often in the habit of going through his correspondence in the evenings. He observed that Ruthvney had not yet done so just prior to dismissing him for the evening. Ruthvney also complained that the chimney was smoking, asking Stevens to remonstrate with Mrs Pritchard, the housekeeper, for what he saw as a lack in her duties. Stevens insists that the chimney was cleaned regularly, indeed it had been done not eight weeks ago. Though he did make the point that as his master insisted on burning a great deal of paper in it, the soot was prone to build up."

Mann looked at Holmes and smiled, pleased to have been able to endorse several of the detective's assumptions.

"Stevens was dismissed at a quarter past eleven, I estimate Ruthvney was dead only a short time later. Say half past the hour, quarter to twelve at the latest. All evidence points to his being left to his own devices for only a short time. He was a voracious drinker and yet the brandy decanter – filled by Stevens that evening – shows only a fifth consumed. The fire was also not built up beyond the state the butler left it in and, as you rightly say, he had time to consult his correspondence and yet not burn it.

"It seems to me that he was disturbed in his reading by someone appearing at the patio door. You will note it was opened at some point in the evening as there are leaf fragments blown in from outside, and I am assured that – whatever the opinion of her master – Mrs Pritchard is fastidious in her duties and would certainly not have allowed a maid to leave such detritus on the carpet."

"So it must have been blown in later, a fair assumption," Holmes said. "What was the weather like here last night? Could the doors have blown open of their own volition?"

"Funny you should ask that," Mann replied, "it was, by every account, a calm night. My house is in fact not far from here and I can assure you that it was a temperate and gentle evening. However, Stevens commented that he heard no noise coming from here after his retiring but that..." Mann consulted his notes so as to be precise, "'given the violence of the storm, the master would have had to make a racket worthy of cannon fire in order to be heard over it.'"

"A storm, eh?" I said. "Not impossible, there could have been a localised bout of bad weather."

"The hall is protected on all sides by trees," Mann said, "plus it is built in a slight dip in the land. If there is a residence more sheltered hereabouts then I don't know of it."

"Your explanation?" Holmes asked.

"I don't have one," Mann admitted. "I've asked the rest of the staff and they all confirm that there was a enough of a storm outside to shake the house to its foundations. A walk in the gardens tells an interesting story also."

Holmes inclined his head. "You are an intriguing fellow, Inspector! Do you wish me to make my own conclusions before you elaborate?"

"All the better to ensure your opinion is objective," Mann said with a broad smile.

Holmes got to his feet. "Then by all means let us walk!"

We left the house via the study, striding across the well-kept lawns in the direction of the forest that faced the rear of the house. Either side of the building was built up into terraces of the sort wealthy landowners like to use to host parties. These terraces were lightly gravelled and monitored by mournful statuary wood nymphs and water-bearing maidens whose shrewish countenances made it clear they would brook no ill behaviour. For all its age and architectural beauty, Ruthvney Hall was a house that made an art out of the death of amusement. It was seriousness personified in every brick, every rectangular window, every perfectly shorn privet hedge. One simply couldn't imagine having a good time there.

It was this prim neatness that ensured the path we had to follow was obvious. Certainly Holmes didn't need encouraging as he set foot upon the wide trail of scattered leaves and branches, a swathe of natural untidiness that seemed to swoop down from the woodland to collide with the bricks of the house itself.

"Remarkable!" I said, stopping in the middle of the lawns to better appreciate the absurdly methodical line of destruction. "I've heard of cyclones of course, particularly in America, but I've never seen anything of the sort here."

"Indeed not," agreed Mann. "But the most bizarre detail is yet to come."

As we reached the edge of the woodland, a mix of evergreens that darkened considerably beyond the periphery, Mann's point became clear.

"It started here," Holmes said, gesturing at a clear circle pressed into the ground as if something heavy had flattened the grass and earth, "then chased forth in a gentle arc towards the house itself."

"You make it sound as though it were alive," I said.

"Yes," he admitted, "or controlled."

"Which is impossible," Mann said.

Holmes nodded. "It is, isn't it? Completely impossible." He tapped at his chin with the crook of his cane, deep in thought. Then he looked up at us both, a big grin on his face. "This is certainly a case worthy of great interest isn't it?"

He began to pace around, scanning the ground. After a few moments he pushed into the forest, eyes always fixed a few feet in front of him as he made his way through the undergrowth.

"On the trail?" I asked, only too aware of the signs that indicated Holmes had a scent in his nostrils.

"As far as I can tell," he replied, "three men gathered around that bizarre circular patch. I'm trying to retrace their steps. A shame our inexplicable wind didn't bring a few rain clouds with it, the ground here is so dry that it's a devil's job to follow their tracks."

I smiled. I knew only too well that Holmes could read every detail, with or without the ease of a muddy surface. I have always placed a complete belief in Holmes' abilities, and for all his occasional announcements of fallibility, I have yet to be disappointed.

"Is there a road near here?" Holmes asked as we got deeper and deeper into the forest.

"Yes," Mann replied, "some way to the east. It's the road we used earlier to get here from the station."

"I thought as much, we will likely find ourselves there before long," Holmes said.

I had moved slightly ahead during their discussion and a glint in the grass ahead of me caught my eye.

"I say! There's something here." I reached for it, gritting my teeth as I scratched my hand and arm on a cluster of brambles that were in the way. As carefully as I could, not wanting to lose all my skin in the attempt, I pulled out a small signet ring. It was onyx with a five-pointed star engraved in white.

"Do be careful with it!" snapped Holmes, reaching for a pair of tweezers.

He pinched it carefully and held it up to the light. "To S.L.M.M.," he said, "engraved on the inside." He dropped the ring into another one of the small envelopes he used to store evidence safely and stepped in front of me. "I'd better stick to the front, I think," he said, jogging ahead. "We don't want you contaminating all the evidence, do we?"

"Thank you, Watson," I muttered under my breath, "a singularly important clue, Watson."

I put on more speed in order to keep up with Holmes, but lost my balance due to the persistent weakness in my left leg (the result of muscle damage cause by a jezail bullet during my time in Afghanistan). With considerable embarrassment I found myself falling onto my side in the dense bracken. Mindful of what an idiot I must look to the following Inspector Mann, I pulled myself to my feet with a defensive bluster. I needn't have made the effort, since quite impossibly I was alone in the forest. Mann had been right behind me, I had been sure of the fact, Holmes only a few feet in front. And yet, turning on the spot, I could see no other soul in that dark forest but me.

As I turned, the meagre light that fell through the thick branches of the pine trees appeared to pulse like the flickering of sunlight on the sea. The repetitive flashing was somehow both terrible and yet compelling, making my head spin. The thick scent of loam came to me and I seemed surrounded entirely by wet rot and the soft, masticating crunch of dead wood and pulped leaves. There was an animal scent there too, perhaps the long-dead cadaver of a fox or badger, its skin dry, its mouth pulled back in that final grin of the corpse. There was a sweet musk of flesh that has liquified and begun to seep into the soil.

It was all I could do not to vomit as all of this assaulted my senses.

I reached out, meaning to steady myself against a tree trunk, to stop this terrible spinning, to find stillness in a world that was moving too fast. My hand connected with the bark and the wet ooze of beetles and worms pressed beneath my palm like grapes exploding in a wine press. Nothing would hold me and nothing would stop the world from revolving around me.

I gave a short cry as I lost my feet once more, toppling onto my back in the undergrowth, feeling its wet leaves and creepers wipe themselves on my cheeks and reach for the wet sustenance of my mouth and eyes.

The ground beneath me continued its motion, rippling like the soft ebb of high tide. I could feel it embracing me, the earth cool and damp as it lapped over my arms and legs, pulling me down into it where I would rot and feed the fat, glistening earthworms that I could swear were exploring my hair. As I sank even lower, what little light there had been vanished as the soil buried me, pulling me deeper and deeper.

Soon I was so far down that I could no longer tell which way led to the surface. Slowly, and with a sharp pain in my chest, I breathed nothing but thick soil and wet clay. I fought to cough the sodden mass from where it clogged my throat but there was nowhere for it to go and I choked. The last sensations, felt just above the pounding in my head, were the touch of the molluscs and beetles that worked their way beneath the folds of my clothes.

"Watson?"

My eyes snapped open at the sound of my friend's voice. I was lying on my back in the undergrowth, both Holmes and Inspector

Mann looking down on me with obvious concern. I confess my embarrassment quite got the better of me and my initial response was somewhat tetchy.

"I'm fine," I retorted, brushing away their hands and pushing myself to my feet.

Utterly disorientated, I looked around, assuming I would determine what had happened in a moment, I just needed to get my bearings... I could still taste soil in my mouth and I rubbed at my face, sure there would be creatures still clinging to me. There were not.

"What happened?" Mann asked.

To my great irritation I simply couldn't provide a satisfactory answer. So I provided a lie. "It was nothing," I said. "I just caught my foot on a root. Shall we carry on?"

I pushed past them both, meaning to force them to continue our pursuit of the trail. I realised almost instantly of course that I could no more lead than explain what had just occurred. Holmes may be able to discern the telltale signs of broken branches and compressed grass but to me their passage was as good as invisible.

Luckily my friend circled around me and took the lead again. He gave me a brief look, as if to ascertain I was all right, then kept his eyes to the ground where the trail was so clear to him it may as well have been painted.

Soon we reached the road we had travelled down earlier. Holmes scouring the verge for further evidence.

"Is it possible to hire a cab from the station?" I wondered aloud.

"Indeed," Mann replied, "though I have already enquired from the station master as to whether any strangers arrived on the late train. He assures me they didn't. This is a quiet area, Dr Watson, and strangers would find it hard work to arrive unnoticed."

"Besides," said Holmes, "if you planned on paying a legitimate visit to the hall you would drive up to the front gate. If your visit was intended to go unnoticed – as their arrival via the forest would certainly suggest – you wouldn't ask a local cab driver to drop you here."

"Yes, all right," I agreed, irritated again. "It was a stupid idea clearly."

"Not at all," Holmes said, giving me a friendly glance. "It was simply a consideration that needed to be addressed and then discounted. It's only by so doing that we get to the truth." He sat down on the verge. "Certainly they did arrive by a small carriage, there are clear grooves in the grass where they pulled off the road a few feet."

"They can't have travelled too far then," Mann said. "Only an idiot would use a horse and carriage for a journey of any great distance."

Holmes shook his head. "Not so much an idiot as a cautious group of men," he said, "one of whom smokes a particularly unusual tobacco."

He scooped a few strands into another empty envelope.

"They had smoked during the journey," he explained, "and knocked out their bowl – most likely on the carriage wheel – here before refilling with enough fresh tobacco to accompany them on their walk through the trees."

"A devoted smoker indeed to feel the need for a pipe on that walk," I said.

Holmes smiled. "Yes, even I managed to avoid tobacco for the duration." He got to his feet. "Right, I don't think we have anything else to learn here. Might I suggest we head back to the station ourselves?"

"You don't wish to interview the servants?" Mann asked, sounding somewhat disappointed.

"Not for now," Holmes replied, "though I will happily read the transcripts of your interviews if you would be so kind as to share? Watson and I have a long journey ahead of us today and I need time to think as well as pack a travel bag."

CHAPTER NINE

TERROR UNDERGROUND

Holmes and I said goodbye to Mann and were soon on a train back to London. I had hoped I might be able to persuade Holmes to allow us lunch at a public house before our journey, but he was resolute that the afternoon held tasks enough that the time could not be allowed. When pressed as to what tasks he had in mind, he would not say. I therefore travelled back in something of an irritated mood. Not helped by a lingering sense of unease after my bizarre episode in the forest. I was still unable to understand what had happened. In my capacity as a doctor I have assisted a number of patients who had experienced fainting spells and blackouts, but try as I might I could pin down none of the obvious symptoms in my case. Unless, of course, it was an early sign of something much worse. Worrying about that wasn't going to help me, however, so I pushed the concern from my mind. After all, it's not as if I didn't know an excellent doctor.

Once we arrived at Liverpool Street, Holmes bade me a goodbye and vanished into the crowds. It was hardly the first time I have been abandoned mid-investigation. Still, with the disorientation of earlier lingering I stood on the streets of the city and felt utterly adrift.

Around me Londoners moved at the only pace they know, hustling to and fro, darting past one another in a complex dance that always reminds me of schools of fish navigating around each other. Stood amongst them I was just another obstacle and was besieged on all sides, both by their impatient shoulders and also by the noise: the constant percussion of hooves on the streets, the shouts of the news vendors, the station announcements behind me. All with that low, bass line of general chatter running underneath it.

For a few moments I felt unable to move, as submerged by the life around me as I had been by the imaginary soil earlier.

What was happening to me? I felt one step removed from the world and unable to drag myself back into the sharp, defined city I knew and loved.

I raised my hands to my head, tapping at my forehead to test for a temperature. My skin was cool.

I wasn't surprised, this didn't feel like an illness. Perhaps I had been poisoned? I thought back to being in Ruthvney's study, trying to imagine when I might have come into contact with something, perhaps even the same chemical that had affected him so markedly. I could think of no way, I had touched nothing, tasted nothing... If it had still been in the air then surely all three of us would have been equally affected?

"You just going to stand there?" asked a voice ahead of me. I looked up to meet the gaze of a news vendor, his ruddy skin a sure sign of years of over-drinking. It began with a wee dram to keep the chill off,

I thought, then you got a real taste for it. "If you do," he continued, "you'll be trod underfoot for sure when the rush hour really starts. You think it's busy now, you just wait until the offices close. Like ants they is, all running for cover."

"I won't be here then," I said, feeling foolish, "just getting my bearings."

"Oh yeah," he replied, "bearings is it? I always keep mine close to hand." With that he proved my earlier guess accurate by removing a hip flask from his pocket, unscrewing the cap and taking a big slug. "Bearings is easy to find if you always keep 'em in the same pocket." He grinned at me and showed two large gaps in his front teeth. Diabetes, the medical man in me decided, probably caused by his diet, or lack of it... He held the hip flask out to me and, somewhat to my own surprise, I moved forward and took it. I drank a mouthful. Cheap rum, that burned rather than warmed. A man of the ocean I decided, revising my opinion, nobody but an ex-sailor would find comfort from this rough stuff. I handed the flask back and checked his wrists for tattoos as he took it from me. Sure enough, the fine curl of a rose stem peered out from beneath his cuff. Rum and tattoos, I thought, if he were any more obvious I would be able to smell the salt.

"Better?" he asked, and despite the roar in my stomach that spoke of indigestion to come I found that the answer was yes and told him so. "I reckon it'll cure almost anything," he said with a knowing twinkle in his eye, "or make it so you don't much care. Liquor's like a politician that way. It don't always fix things but it makes sure you don't notice what's broke."

"You might benefit from a square meal to soak some of it up every now and then," I told him.

"Yes, doctor," he said and for a moment I studied his face, nonsensically believing it might be Holmes in disguise. Of course it wasn't, Holmes was about better business than this.

"Look after yourself," I told him and walked off into the crowd.

Unlike my friend I did not have a bottomless bank account so I took the underground train rather than a cab.

The experience of descending beneath the streets into the tiled corridors of the underground stations is one that is both alarming and invigorating. There can be few that are not impressed with our capital's subterranean travel system. As limited and restrictive as it may currently be, there is no doubt in my mind that it will one day expand, triumphing over its initial difficulties to become the preferred method for all. Its detractors point to thirty years of staggered development and the king's ransom that's been ploughed into it. When will they just give up? they wonder. But in my experience that's something that the British in general and Londoners in particular have never been very good at. It's just not in our nature to accept defeat – we bang our heads against a problem until it has the good grace to acquiesce.

Soon they say the lines will be filled with the new electric carriages, strange beasts that whine endlessly as they carry themselves to and fro beneath the city. Until then we are stuck with steam trains and the air in the tunnels is as poisonous as if we were burrowing through an alien world.

I worked my way through the crowds towards my platform, the thick smell of smoke and sweat clinging to me as I stood waiting for the next train.

I held onto my hat as the wind began to build, forced along the tunnels by the train as it approached.

"Enough to knock you off your feet so it is!" cackled a woman to my right. I offered her a polite smile as she eyed me up. Judging by the state of her painted face it was clear that she considered me a potential client. She gave a grin that showed yellow teeth stained by carmine lipstick, the smile of a clown or a cannibal. She pushed down her skirts as the wind grew even stronger, as if afraid they may blow up around her. I looked away, on the off chance that she was right.

A young couple stood hand in hand, a handsome pair, on a day trip I guessed. They had that awkward air of a fresh couple, excitement tempered by nerves. It made me think of my darling Mary, now lost to me, and I was somewhat ashamed to realise my eyes were watering as the oncoming train's whistle howled. "Your feelings are showing, John," she would have said, reaching out to dry the tears with a soft, gloved thumb. Like Holmes, she had always accused me of keeping my emotions so close to the surface you could read them from a mile away. I couldn't argue with her, it was true enough. But then what Holmes frequently saw as a failure she saw as an asset. I am as yet undecided as to my own opinion on the matter.

The train pulled into the station and we climbed aboard. Sitting down on the upholstered bench, I looked at the wooden panelling of the carriage and was uncomfortably reminded of the inside of a coffin, all walnut, velvet and sweet, damp earth.

The young couple sat down across from me. The doxy a few feet to my left, a puff of cheap lavender toilet water erupting from the folds of her clothes as she rearranged herself on the seat. In front of her an ageing minister, his grey-and-white curls bobbing around his pink face as the train began its shaky journey, scanned the pages of his well-worn bible. Every now and then his lips quivered as he read the words, a soft, sibilant noise coming from him, like a dying breath, as he nearly spoke aloud. An elderly lady sat next to him, picking at loose threads in her bonnet, her face was vacant and dreamy as if she imagined herself to be anywhere but here. At the end of the carriage a pair of young lads laughed and cuffed each other playfully, standing up to "ride" the unsteady train as it shook on the rails.

I closed my eyes, and listened to the rattle of the wheels on the track, the eager chuffing of the engine as it ate its coke and its heart blazed hot within its iron cage. I could imagine it as a voracious creature, consuming all it could swallow, burrowing through the earth, a never-ending beast of appetite.

"It will kill us all," said the doxy and I opened my eyes to look at her. She writhed against the bench as if being tugged by invisible hands, her back arched, her mouth opening and closing as if eating the air. "It will blow hard and sweep us from the earth," she continued, "the Breath of God cannot be stopped, it curls hot in the lungs of the world."

"Is nobody to help her?" I asked, reaching across to hold her thrashing arms.

"There is no help," said the old minister, as if reading the words from his bible, "we're all going to burn."

"Let her die," said the young couple, in impossible harmony, their eyes rolled up into their sockets, their mouths flapping open in perfect unison to let the words tumble out. "She is a harlot and not worth our attention, she deserves no more than the touch of hot pokers, the searing, cleansing fire on her diseased body."

I continued to wrestle with the prostitute, made all the more determined by the callous words behind me.

"Oh God, John," she said, and it was Mary's voice, my poor dead Mary. "I can feel their hands, feel their black nails piercing the skin. Can nothing be done to save me?"

"Mary!" I cried, delirious now in the confined carriage that burrowed itself deeper and deeper into the ground.

"She's ours," said one of the young boys.

"We will play with her until she breaks," agreed the other as they walked over to join us, "your little rag doll, your little Mary."

The train shook violently and I lost my footing, letting go of the woman who had my deceased wife's voice trapped inside her. I fell to the floor, rolling towards the far window as the carriage continued to buck and shake.

"Beware!" cried the old woman, unspooling great strands from her bonnet, strands I now realised were red and wet as she peeled herself like a Christmas orange. "Beware!"

Everyone on the carriage stood up, their mouths opening to reveal great black holes like the tunnels through which we travelled. Out of those tunnels a wind began to blow, whistling past teeth, billowing out cheeks, swelling their bodies to absurd, distorted balloons as it filled them.

The carriage filled with the unnatural wind, a wind that brought on its back the smell of the grave and of the bloodstained mud of the battlefields of my youth. It was the percussive wind of cannon fire, the raging storm pushed before the explosion of gunpowder, the storm of death, and I couldn't bear the thought of inhaling it. If it entered me, contaminated my body with its funeral taint, I was convinced I would be forever lost.

I pulled myself to my feet, yanked down the window and breathed deep of the black smoke that flooded the carriage.

"'E's gone mad!" someone shouted, and that was enough to bring me back to my senses. The hands of the young man yanked me back from the window even as the old minister pulled it closed, coughing in the clouds of smoke that I had allowed into the carriage from the confined tunnel outside.

It was one of the young lads who had spoken and I held my hands up, trying to reassure my travelling companions that I was now as restored to sanity as they clearly had been. But they knew nothing of my delusions, that much was clear from the startled looks on their faces. They were all sat as they had been before I had closed my eyes, looking on me with a mixture of terror and pity. My eyes met those of the prostitute and there was no trace of Mary in their open mockery.

"Could tell 'e weren't right the minute I set eyes on 'im," she said, looking me up and down with open contempt as the train slowed to pull into the next station. "'E's like a man I used to know." A client, I thought, perhaps uncharitably. "Used to scream the 'ouse down on a full moon so he did, right off his onion, mad as Swiss eggs."

As the train came to a halt I grabbed my hat and cane and dismounted, unable to travel any further with them, too embarrassed to sit in their company. I pushed my way past the people wanting to get on and made a run for the surface. I still coughed, the sharp sting of blood at the back of my throat, the thick, poisonous smoke clinging to my insides.

I came up near Regent's Park and I made my way there, to sit a while on one of the benches and regain my breath and composure.

Had I fallen asleep? No. I was sure I had not. Then what was the explanation for two such experiences in one day? What was happening to me? I was only too aware of the similarity between what I had experienced and the surreal visions described by Dr Silence. Had I been influenced by him somehow or – a much worse proposition and one that did not sit well with my rationalist beliefs – had we shared a similar visitation? I resolved to observe Dr Silence later that evening and try to make my mind up about him.

Eventually I walked through the park and along Baker Street. I would tell Holmes about what had happened – he would treat the account with utter scepticism, naturally, but I was hopeful that he might be able to present a logical solution. Try as I might, I certainly couldn't.

On my return, it soon became clear that conversation with Holmes would have to wait. He had returned home while I was out, a note pinned to the mantelpiece with a blowdart: "Meet at the station, bring your revolver."

Typically erudite, I thought, screwing the note up and casting it into the fire.

I went to pack.

CHAPTER TEN

Journeying North

With a small holdall packed (my old service revolver wrapped snugly in a clean shirt), I made my way to St Pancras and the rendez vous with Holmes and Silence. My experience on the Underground still fresh, I decided to forgo the saving to my purse and hire a cab.

The station was as busy as always. I dislike train stations, they are full of lost people, running here and there, fearful of missing their connections. It is a contagious atmosphere of confusion and dread and I'm always relieved when my train pulls away from the platform.

I stood in the queue to purchase my ticket. I had adequate time to reach the platform but the impatience bred of waiting soon affected me and I was tapping my foot as an elderly lady craned her neck so as to face her least defective ear towards the guard, all the better to hear him with.

"Inverness," she shouted, so that none of us were in any doubt as to her destination. "I can't manage all these bags though."

"I'll gladly help with your bags," I insisted, if only to get things moving. The old lady looked at me and there was a distinct twinkle to her eye as she gently pressed her hands together as if in prayer.

"Such a kind gentleman," she said and I couldn't help but smile. I remembered the time when, running for our lives, Holmes and I had arranged to meet on the continental train from Victoria. I had believed my friend to be absent until an ageing cleric sat across from me revealed himself to be Holmes in disguise. I was certainly not to be fooled twice.

"When you've quite finished," said a young man behind me. I turned to look at the fellow, immaculately dressed with hair so perfectly oiled he could have been sculpted. He checked his pocket watch, a gleaming half-hunter with an arcane-looking symbol etched onto the back. "She's not the only one who would like to make the next train to Inverness."

"Indeed not," I replied, "I'm travelling there myself."

"Such an optimist," the young man replied holding out his watch for me to see, "it leaves in ten minutes. Do you think you and your lady friend may have concluded your business by then?"

"What's he saying?" the old lady asked – if indeed she *was* an old lady.

"No matter," I replied, eager to have the whole affair done with. "Could you please supply me with two tickets for Inverness?" I asked the guard. "One for this lady and one for myself."

"Thank you," said the old lady. "If you could bring my bags too, young man."

With that she wandered off across the concourse leaving me stood face to face with the guard and in charge of one leather suitcase and three hatboxes. It *must* be Holmes, I thought, no-one else would have the damned gall to abandon me in such a manner.

"I say..." I called after the retreating old lady, but she was either too deaf or too content with her own good fortune to hear me.

It *must* be Holmes.

"Now nine minutes," said the young man behind me.

"For goodness' sake." I paid for the tickets and gathered up the bags. If that wasn't my friend then I was now sorely out of pocket and fast losing patience.

I shuffled after the elderly figure, managing to reach our platform after only dropping the hatboxes once.

Silence was hanging out of the window of one of the carriages, clearly convinced that neither Holmes nor I intended to keep the appointment.

"Dr Watson!" he called, opening the door and stepping down to help me with my burden. "I fear I may have packed too lightly," he said, casting his eyes over the baggage.

"It's not mine," I insisted, calling to the elderly figure who was shuffling along to the far end of the train.

"We should sit near the front," it called, "my grandson says that's safest."

"You know this lady?" Silence asked.

"I have a terrible suspicion I do," I replied. "Come on, we'll move up."

Silence grabbed his overnight case and the hatboxes and we walked along the platform, breaking into a slight jog as the conductor whipped his flag in preparation for the train departing.

"Get on!" I shouted at the figure. "This is far enough, surely?"

"No need to shout, dear," she replied, pulling at the door handle and struggling to clamber aboard. Just as it looked as though she was going to fall back onto the platform a pair of arms shot out of the open doorway and grasped her firmly.

"Holmes?" I asked, staring at the familiar figure helping the elderly lady aboard.

"Watson!" he replied, "I was beginning to fear you would miss the train, now I see that chivalry delayed you both."

We all climbed aboard and I set to wedging the old lady's belongings on the baggage rack.

"How on earth did you end up travelling en masse?" asked Holmes, taking a hatbox from me and putting it away.

"I..." I considered lying but decided against it, knowing Holmes would catch me out. "I thought she was you in disguise."

Holmes erupted into laughter, clapping his hands and ushering Silence and I from the carriage. "If you need anything else, madam," he told the lady, "don't hesitate to call on my friend, we'll be in the next carriage along."

"Wait a moment," I said, thinking of the rail fare.

"Don't mind me," the old lady said. "It's most kind I'm sure, but I can't have you pestering me all the way to Scotland, you get on with your business and leave me in peace."

I stared at her, dumbfounded, before following a still-laughing Holmes out into the corridor and towards the next carriage.

"I'm flattered," said Holmes, "that you think I could pull off such a convincing impersonation."

"It has been a trying day."

"The last few minutes seem to have been hard enough, poor chap. Let's hope this interminable journey gives you adequate time to recover."

"As long as there's comfortable seats and a restaurant carriage, I assure you I will arrive north of the border in fine fettle."

We sat down and Holmes filled his pipe.

"So," he said, once relaxed and beginning to fill the carriage with the clouds of Turkish tobacco smoke, "perhaps we might best spend the time between now and dinner by catching up on what we've been up to since this morning."

For Dr Silence's benefit he then began to inform him of what we had learned at Ruthvney Hall, up to and including my "turn" in the forest.

"I'm sure there's a perfectly simple – and quite benign – medical explanation for it," I said, aware even as I spoke of how pompous and silly I sounded. In truth I felt even more foolish now it was being discussed in front of Silence. I felt like the weak heroine of a pulp tale fainting at suitably dramatic points within the narrative.

"Well then perhaps we could avail ourselves of an expert opinion?" asked Holmes. "In fact a qualified second opinion." He looked to Silence.

The man, no doubt sensing my discomfort, attempted to back away from the challenge. "I'm quite sure that if Dr Watson, as a medical man himself, is at ease with what happened..."

"Oh come now!" said Holmes. "You're a doctor, you must have met countless intelligent patients who attempt to dismiss important symptoms through a misguided sense of embarrassment?"

"I am sat here you know, Holmes," I muttered, irritated as ever by my friend's inability to consider the feelings of others.

"Indeed you are," he replied, utterly unabashed, "and not denying a word. Has something similar happened since?"

"It was nothing, Holmes, I..." But that had done it hadn't it? And indeed it was stupid to remain silent, as foolish as I might have felt, the truth was that I had now twice suffered from a delusional blackout. Both times preyed upon by the most insidious and terrifying visions. That was just the sort of thing, speaking as a medical man, that was not to be lightly dismissed. "It happened again while travelling on the Underground," I admitted, proceeding to tell them, in as much detail as I could remember, what I had seen and heard.

Holmes, for all his bluster and insensitivity, had the grace to look ashamed when I recounted how I had heard my dead wife's voice. Though his sense of shame was swiftly eradicated by interest when I had passed on the message I had been given.

"Fascinating!" he said. "A story which bears no small similarity to the one you told us only a couple of days ago," he said to Silence.

"Indeed," agreed Silence, "it would be my opinion that the Doctor was prey to a visitation of spirits."

"Oh, rubbish," I insisted. "It was no such thing, it was simply a delusion brought about by... by..." But in my defence, I could come up with no solution. Which made me angrier still. I felt I was being backed into a corner.

"Well," said Holmes, "whatever it was remains to be seen, but we would be foolish to ignore the information passed on. After all," he glanced at Silence, "what the voices chose to impart to you was of great relevance."

"But surely there was nothing of the remotest use," I said, still wishing we could drop the subject.

"Very little," Holmes agreed, "which strikes me as exceedingly interesting..."

As the afternoon faded to evening outside the window of our compartment, my thoughts turned once more to the dining carriage. In truth it was as much to get some fresh air as it was to eat – Holmes kept the windows closed while he smoked, insisting the dense atmosphere helped him to concentrate. Medically speaking it helped me do nothing but cough, so it was with some relief that, when I suggested we take a stroll, Silence agreed to accompany me while Holmes remained.

"I have my thoughts to sustain me," he said, gazing out of the window at the silhouettes of trees as they flashed by. "I'm sure they will be more nourishing than whatever the hard-pressed chefs of the North-Eastern Railway can provide."

When Silence and I entered the dining carriage I was momentarily worried by the sight of the troublesome old lady from earlier. However, she appeared to have latched on to some other unfortunate, a rather pale-faced man who had the waistcoat and creased brow of a clerk.

"He would insist on following me," she was telling him while noisily consuming her consommé by inhalation. "In the end I had to tell the fellow to leave me be."

I resisted a brief, ungentlemanly urge to tip her soup into her wool-enshrouded lap, but instead led Silence to the other end of the carriage where we might just be able to eat without hearing her do so.

I sat with my back to her, briefly catching the eye of the immaculate young man who had been stood behind me in the ticket queue. He gave me a desultory glance before returning to his lamb. I had always considered myself a convivial man but it would seem I had managed to make a pair of enemies without any effort whatsoever. Perhaps it was that thought that made me decide to relax in Silence's company.

It wasn't difficult, while not a man overly blessed with a sense of humour, he was nonetheless pleasant and capable of charm. He could hardly have been a successful physician otherwise, any successful doctor will tell you a practice is built on charm as much as medical knowledge.

As doctors cannot fail to do when placed in each other's company, we shared stories of our training days. We had not been at St Bartholomew's at the same time, but nonetheless knew a good number of the same people and conversation was easy and pleasant.

However much shared history we possessed, it wasn't long before discussion of Silence's more recent work was broached.

"How did you end up specialising in such an..."

"Unbelievable?"

I smiled. "I was going to say unconventional."

Silence shrugged. "Once you are convinced of the existence of – for the sake of a term – 'the supernatural' it is difficult to ignore it. It feels as if you have peeled away an entirely new layer of existence, everything you took for granted, every physical law or spiritual belief, is turned on its head. Once you believe, and I mean truly believe, it's impossible to dedicate your life to anything else. I'm hardly the first."

"Really?"

"Not at all, Dr Martin Hesselius pursued a dual career in both medicine and the occult long before me. You're familiar with his work?"

I had to admit that I was not.

"Very few have heard of him, which speaks volumes for how little he was respected by conventional science." He sighed. "Though perhaps that is hardly surprising – pioneers are always thought of as mad. A great deal of his work was research only; he studied myths and legends, trying to sift truth from fiction. He also fought the unearthly face to face, as of course did his successor Lawrence Van Helsing."

"Now that is a name I am familiar with," I said, "though some of the details elude me. Wasn't he involved in some trouble in Eastern Europe?"

"Lawrence has been involved in trouble the world over," Silence admitted. "For such a mild-mannered fellow, he is the most tenacious man I think I have ever met. Of course he has specialised rather, whereas I prefer to keep my scope of interests wide. A good man though, I spent a number of months in Chungking recently working alongside Van Helsing and his protegé Charles Kent."

"You have travelled extensively then?"

"Oh yes, the world has much to teach us, but to learn you have to walk its roads."

"An enlightened philosophy."

"And one I am lucky that I can afford to subscribe to. Life has treated me well."

As someone who often struggled to pay the rent on his practice – indeed had been forced to return to sharing rooms in order to meet the bills – I was forced to agree. I didn't allow such thoughts of penury to dissuade my attentions from the dessert trolley, however – a man has to live you know.

"There is something..." Dr Silence's words petered out mid-sentence and I gazed up from my slice of gateau to look at him. His face had become peculiarly inanimate. His lower lip sagged and a wisp of what I first took to be smoke but then, discerning its slick, glutinous texture as it dripped on the table linen, realised was something else entirely.

"Dr Silence?" I asked. "John?"

There was no answer, what sat before me was an empty vessel.

For a moment I feared that I had, once again, fallen prey to a delusional state. Though if I had then it was one that the rest of the carriage shared. Silence wasn't alone in having lost all semblance of life, I glanced from table to table seeing the same blank expressions dotted among the diners, their companions as confused as I. All exuded that same, thin mucous-like substance, strings of it reaching up from their mouths and nostrils and forming a web between their heads and the walls of the carriage.

Taking hold of my dessert knife I extended the blade towards the closest string, meaning to test its strength.

"Don't touch it," said the immaculate young man I had first met in the ticket queue. He turned to the carriage as a whole. "None of you touch it," he shouted. "Do as I say and stay calm and we might yet get out of this."

"And you are?" I asked, not a little set back by his arrogance.

"An expert," he replied. "The name's Thomas Carnacki."

CHAPTER ELEVEN

INTERLUDE: THE ACCOUNT OF THOMAS CARNACKI

It's morning and I open the windows to exchange the smell of stale cigar smoke for the crisp morning breeze and a hint of the Thames.

I sit amongst the detritus of the night before, the brandy glasses and empty decanter, the full ashtrays and the scent of a mutton stew prepared in the Moroccan style. The smell of spice and smoke is not the only ghost to still linger. Last night I told Dodgson and the others of the bizarre affair of Mocata Grange, of a world glimpsed beyond this one.

As always the story aided their digestion even as it complicated mine.

They love my stories of course, even those of them who suspect me of embellishment. For me the act of reliving my cases is not simply an after-dinner entertainment, that is what they will never quite understand. For me it's about fixing the impossible, taking the unearthly and the horrific and pinning it down like a gassed butterfly.

As I tell my story and Dodgson notes it down it becomes a thing shared, a thing diluted by the echo of nervous laughter, something crystallised in the ink of Dodgson's pen. In short it is something taken out of my head and laid down where one must hope it can no more harm me. Or keep me from sleep.

I need air. Leaving the tidying up for later I put on my coat and scarf and leave my flat for the crisp winter air of Cheyne Walk.

I walk by the river. The early sun throws its light on the water but sheds none of its warmth. My breath clouds in front of my face as I look across the narrow mud flats at the feeding gulls. I am reminded of my current investigation. I am reminded of the Breath of God.

It is not something I have discussed with Dodgson and friends, they only get to hear of the adventures I have concluded. The works in progress are too dangerous to share, they are snakes as yet loose from their basket. I will capture them, close the lid and then take away their poison by speaking of them out loud. Until then...

After my walk I return to my flat and wash the dishes. I could employ someone to do this, my inheritance is such that money need never be a significant concern, but about the only thing I like more than privacy is self-sufficiency.

Once the flat is cleared, I turn my attentions to the future: I begin the preparations for my planned journey.

The first step is simple, I gather my notebooks, a map of the local area and a suitable change of clothes. Next comes the equipment, and that is a more careful business, the electric Pentacle is carefully checked and then replaced in its padded case. I also run through my Gladstone bag filled with a selection of useful tools, such basic equipment as holy water and communion wafers, a selection of silver charms and a handful of crystals. There is also my revolver, with a choice of cartridges: silver, rock salt or standard rounds (it is saddening how often the threats I face are only too earthly). Then there are the sections of the Sigsand Manuscript that I have gathered over the years, a scroll so potent that it is not only the words that hold power – words I have long since memorised – but the very fabric of the parchment itself.

Finally comes mental preparation and this is not something that can be achieved so quickly. First, purification: bathing then oiling, then shaving and finally bathing again. By the time I sit, cross-legged, in my meditation space I am pink skinned and icy cold. After a few moments of chanting, however, the flesh is left behind and the mental preparation begins. I compartmentalise, visualising my mind as a massive storeroom, all that I know is unpacked, regarded and then filed away again, perfectly neatly. By the time I open my eyes the morning has gone and I need to get moving.

I dress and quickly eat a little leftover curried turkey (I do so love to cook, good food is like successful magic, it's all in the ingredients and the willingness to be brave). Then I gather my bags and take the car to St Pancras. I am tempted to drive all the way – that need for self-sufficiency again, I do so hate to rely on others – but the train journey will give me time to catch up on my reading and leave me refreshed when I arrive in Scotland, rather than grimy from the road.

I join the queue at the ticket office, almost giving up entirely when stuck behind a lady so ancient I can recall battling spirits more youthful. Her companion is scant help, though I feel sure I recognise him. Glancing at my watch – a truly lovely piece that I've had engraved with the mark of the Kronos Lineage so that it is not only a fine example of Swiss timekeeping but also a formidable weapon against Succubi – I realise I am now in a very real danger of missing my train. Given the hours of preparation I've put into planning my trip I can't say I'm favourable to the idea of it being scuppered by a lunatic octogenarian and her companion. I hurry them along and finally manage to buy my ticket and reach the platform with only minutes to spare.

I spot a couple of familiar faces as I board and am momentarily undecided whether their presence will present a complication or a benefit. First there is John Silence, a man who works roughly in the same field as myself (though in a considerably less active manner; from what I gather he is a man who likes to listen rather than act). The second could also be classed as competition, though I believe he restricts his detective work to the earthly, Sherlock Holmes, the renowned consulting detective. Of course, I now realise where I recognised the elderly lady's companion, he was John Watson, Holmes' biographer. What he was doing escorting those on the cusp of death cannot be imagined.

Can it be possible that their presence is coincidence? Or are they perhaps following the same trail as I?

Settling into my carriage with a small pile of research material beside me, I decide that time alone will tell.

Once my eyes are too tired to decipher further dusty apocrypha, I pack the books away and see about food. There is a dining carriage onboard and, while experience has taught me not to set one's hopes too high when eating on the move, I am glad enough of the opportunity to stretch my legs.

I take a table and a gamble on the menu. The food is actually better than I had expected, a goose paté in particular being almost worthy of the wine I choose to wash it down with.

The doctors, Silence and Watson, enter and I consider making conversation in order to determine the reason for their visit. Then I decide I really can't tear myself away from the wine and dessert course. Small talk has never been something that I relish.

It is as I am finally resolving to return to my carriage, with a plan to meditate for a couple of hours before we arrive, that the incursion occurs. First the temperature drops, I seem to be one of the few that notice, the rest no doubt caught up in their oh-so-fascinating conversations. A small patch of ice forms in the corner of my window, like a spider's web. I hold out my finger to touch it: it's on the outside, so whatever is affecting us is sizeable and likely enveloping this entire carriage. The degree of psionic energy needed to achieve such a manifestation is daunting. Of course, I have left all of my equipment in my carriage, only a paranoid dines with his weaponry.

I am considering a sprint to retrieve my Gladstone bag when roughly half of the passengers are struck by a spiritual attack. They fall silent, heads lolling back while an ectoplasmic bridge begins to form, its gooey threads providing a conduit between the life force of the affected passengers and whatever creature this is that wishes to manifest. That solves the question of power, I realise, we are victims and power source both.

I notice Watson making to break one of the ectoplasm strings with his cake knife. Save me from amateurs.

"Don't touch it," I tell him, getting to my feet and hoping I can alert the whole carriage to the same need for caution. "None of you touch it," I shout. "Do as I say and stay calm and we might yet get out of this."

"And you are?" Watson asks, clearly irritated.

"An expert," I reply, truthfully and succinctly. "The name's Thomas Carnacki."

Out of the corner of my eye I spot the same irritating old lady I was stuck behind in the ticket queue, the woman I assumed to be Watson's companion. She is reaching out to touch one of the ectoplasmic strands hanging from the corner of her dinner companion's mouth. "I said don't touch it!" I cry, but it's too late, her fingers are already breaking the fragile connection.

The man in front of her begins to shake as the force outside the carriage seeks to regain its lost connection. The ectoplasm pulses and whips back around his face, obscuring his startled moment of wakefulness and choking a brief scream as it yanks him upwards. The man collides with the roof of the carriage, spinning as the ectoplasm curls around him. There is a faint cracking noise as his soul is yanked from the flesh that houses it. The body falls, utterly empty, back to the dining table where it overturns a pot of coffee. The soul is swallowed by the ectoplasm, which bulges as the vaguely luminescent morsel passes along it, like a rabbit in the throat of a python.

The old lady is quite beside herself, wailing with fear. Then she faints. A mercy for us all.

"I trust I don't have to repeat myself?" I say. "If you touch it, you will kill the person it is attached to. Do not even move, you do not want to attract its attention in case it decides to attach itself to you. Do not speak because I am trying to concentrate and, as I am certainly your best chance at getting off this train alive, you want to give me your greatest consideration."

"Insufferable man," I hear Watson mutter. And I can't help but smile. He is, after all, quite right. Still, he will be forgiving enough in the end I imagine, should I deal with whatever it is that has set its sights on us.

The carriage begins to shake slightly, though whether the effect of the creature outside or a simple matter of irregular track I can't as yet guess. The windows are dark, no great surprise given the hour. However, the longer I look at them, the more I realise that it isn't simply a case of night having fallen. They are *totally* dark, no lights from towns, no stars. I begin to wonder if the world is still to be found outside these four thin walls.

"I'm going to move slowly along the carriage," I announce, feeling I need to keep my fellow passengers informed in case they suddenly panic, run and doom us all.

The ectoplasmic web begins to move slightly, the whole, gelatinous construction swaying with a movement that again puts me in mind of a snake: that slow dance of a cobra's head as it follows the bell of his charmer's pipe.

When I speak again it is only in a whisper. "It is aware of me," I say, "but if I move slowly it shouldn't strike. At the moment it is fed, it sustains without me, if I become too obvious, however, it may become greedy. Please, the rest of you, don't agitate it further."

I slide my feet along the carpet, shuffling slowly forward like an ice skater, determined to make as little overt movement as possible. Soon I am near the connecting door.

"You're not leaving us?" comes a frail voice from behind me, a woman sat next to her ectoplasm-strewn husband.

"I need to see what's on the other side of that door," I reply. "Just stay calm and wait."

"You are!" she says. "You're running away!"

She begins to get to her feet and the web moves, a thick tentacle forming that grasps at her hands and feet. She wails as it pulls her out of her seat and towards the roof.

"Carnacki, man!" shouts Watson, ever the heroic type, he cannot watch a woman in peril. "Do something!"

He also rises and, in a moment I realise the control I have over these people will be gone. I run the last couple of feet to the door and yank it open, aware that the web has now turned its attention to me. I see it move in the reflection of the window, I sense its attention on the back of my neck. Any moment now it will reach for me and then we'll all be doomed.

Beyond the door there is just as I feared: nothing, a great, interminable blackness. Knowing I can hardly retreat I do the only thing I can: I step out of the door.

I grasp the small ladder to the left of me and pull myself up and onto the roof of the carriage. This small part of the train, though now removed from its fellow carriages, still rattles along what it can remember of the track and it takes not inconsiderable skill on my part to retain my balance. I am fortunate in that there is no wind to drag me off, though certainly something is out here with me and, as I stand in the centre of the roof and look up, I can sense its terrible eye gazing down on me. I can't quite discern its shape, which is not unusual for an incursion of this nature. The creatures that move beyond our reality are bound to none of our physical laws, they have forms and dimensions that are so beyond our frame of reference that the brain struggles to cope. There is a shimmer of colour, like a reflection in the surface of crude oil, a shifting of matter that creaks, swelling to the limit of its mantels and joists. Something sinks down towards me, a long proboscis that glistens like offal.

I begin to recite the opening lines of the Sigsand Manuscript. Without the parchment itself the effect is drastically reduced, though it buys me the time to loosen my bow-tie and undo my collar. I can sense it creeping closer, brushing away the ancient words of power as nothing more than an irritation. I fling my dinner jacket upwards and feel a peppering of dust on my face as it is destroyed by a touch of this infernal creature's tongue. I palm my cufflinks (they were a gift from my mother, inlaid with the bone fragments of St Benedict and far too precious to just hurl into the void) then tear off my shirt. My skin burns in the rarified atmosphere of the abyss, this fragile barrier between realities, and my chest – or rather the sigils tattooed into it – begin to glow.

Only an idiot doesn't prepare himself for anything in my line of work and I have spent a painful six months building the most extensive and elaborate system of protective tattoos. Using ink blessed by a Catholic priest of my frequent acquaintance I am wearing a combination of runes and Chinese protection sigils that, thanks to the gift of transubstantiation, are effectively drawn in the blood of Christ. If that's not a potent bit of protective magic, I don't know what is.

The air above me quivers and the shift in pressure makes my eardrums pop and ache as the massive body of whatever it was that loomed over me slips back to where it came from, withdrawing its ectoplasmic net and its presence in our world. Of course, the moment it does so, our train is fully back in the "real" world and the wall of air that hits me, the slipstream caused by the train's speed as it races along the track, knocks me off my feet.

CHAPTER TWELVE

A Fold in Reality

It is an experience that frequently returns to me, even after everything else that happened. That carriage, the hellish web of what Carnacki later informed me was ectoplasm, a by-product of spiritual interference, of the invasion from one reality to another. To a rational man, a man who had always held strong to his beliefs in a solid world, a world that had no place for the table rappers and carnival palm readers, it was an assault on the mind as well as the body.

The young woman, panic stripping her of all common sense, had made a break for the door, believing that Carnacki meant to abandon rather than help us.

"Carnacki, man!" I had shouted. "Do something!" But it was clear that he felt intervention beyond him as he vanished from the carriage.

As the glutinous strands of ectoplasm reached for her, I made the decision that, whether or not I understood what was happening, I could no longer be a bystander to it. The woman would not come to harm if I could help it. I have never been a man that can stand by when others are in danger. Had that not been the case I probably would have avoided the bullet wound that pensioned me off from the army in the first place,

"Hold on!" I shouted to her. "Help is coming!"

I doubt such naïve offerings consoled her much but, grabbing a meat fork from the waiter's serving trolley, I leaped upon the woman's table and thrust its thick, steel tines into the ectoplasm. It was like attacking a jellyfish with a stick, counterproductive and likely to end in the aggressor being stung.

The ectoplasm formed a new strand which wrapped itself around my waist. For all its apparent lack of substance, when it constricted, my breath was forced from my body and I imagined my ribs might break were it to squeeze any tighter. I tore at the thing with the meat fork but the jelly simply reformed as quickly as I could tear a furrow in it. I felt hands grip my ankles as a fellow passenger sought to yank me free.

"Never mind me!" I shouted. "Grab the lady!"

People were already trying, but as much as they pulled at us, they too were grasped by the slick tentacles. In a matter of moments the whole carriage was a screaming mess of juddering ectoplasm and passengers desperate for their lives.

Those that had originally been captured in the web began to shake violently. Carnacki had said the thing was feeding, had the exertion demanded it drain even more energy from its prey? If so could they survive the experience or would they follow the same, presumed fate of the poor man we had watched flung aside a few moments ago?

It would seem there was little I could hope to do about it, in fact, as the tentacle's grip tightened, my vision began to blur and I realised I was close to passing out.

Then, with no warning, the ectoplasm vanished, and we all found ourselves back in our seats.

"Dear Lord," I whispered, looking at Silence, "did that even happen or was I...?"

He held a hand to his temple, face crumpled in pain. "It happened," he said, "I can still taste the after-effects in the air."

There was a resounding crack and Carnacki, bare-chested, appeared outside our window, clearly hanging on for dear life.

I pulled down the window and Silence and I grabbed the young man by the shoulders and pulled him inside.

"How on earth did you end up out there?" I asked.

"Battling the infernal, as per usual," he replied, lifting my wine glass and draining it of its contents.

"I say, sir!" cried the young lady whom I had risked the continued solidity of my ribs to rescue. She showed no sign of distress from her encounter, in fact the only emotion clearly on display was one of indignation. "Do you really think that is suitable attire in a mixed dining carriage?" she asked.

I looked to my colleagues in some confusion. "I'm sorry?"

She flicked her fingers towards Carnacki's bare chest. "I can assure you 'gentlemen,'" and the sarcastic stress she placed on that word was only too clear, "he is as scantily dressed as my salad and twice as unwelcome while I'm eating. Please retire to your carriage and avail yourself of a shirt at the very least."

"Madam," I replied, "do you not think there are more important things to concern ourselves with than the sight of some pectoral muscles?"

"And fine pectoral muscles they are too," muttered Carnacki.

"They are as tanned and tattooed as a maritime thug, sir," she replied, "and it sickens me to look upon them. I fail to see what can be more important to a gentleman, if indeed there are any in attendance, than the feelings of a lady. Kindly retire."

"But madame..."

There was a scream from the far end of the carriage and our attention was drawn to the elderly lady who was still in my debt to the tune of one rail fare to Inverness.

"He's dead!" she cried, pointing at the middle-aged clerk sat across from her. "And I was only just talking to him!"

"Well, of course..." I began to say before Silence gripped my arm and pulled me back.

"They don't remember," he said, "none of them have the slightest idea what just happened."

"But how can that be?" I asked as Silence made his way to the other end of the carriage to console the elderly lady and check on the state of her dinner companion.

"It's more common than you would credit," said Carnacki, "I've seen entire households ignore the most grotesque supernatural incursions simply because their rational minds cannot accept it. Either that or reality itself has been folded back as a direct result of the beast's departure."

He pulled his watch from his trouser pocket and checked the dial. "Could that be it?" he asked himself. "The entire event expunged from our personal timelines?"

"I haven't the slightest idea what you're talking about," I told him. "If they have forgotten then how come we remember? It makes not a jot of sense."

Carnacki smiled. "Welcome to my working life, Doctor. It puts missing diamonds and homicidal dowagers in their place somewhat, doesn't it?"

Silence returned. "Dead from heart failure," he said quietly, "with no external signs of anything untoward."

"Nothing to corroborate what just happened?" I asked.

"Nothing," he replied. "I must talk to the conductor."

"Good evening, gentlemen," came a voice along the gangway. "I hope I haven't missed service?" I looked up to see Holmes striding towards us. He stopped in his tracks, the shock in our faces – not to mention Carnacki's state of undress – giving him pause. "Ah," he said momentarily. "I see that perhaps I have."

CHAPTER THIRTEEN

A Meeting in Bloomsbury

We all retired from the dining carriage. Carnacki strolled off towards his own compartment agreeing to rejoin us once he had improved his appearance to the tune of a shirt and collar.

For myself I had an almost overpowering urge to console myself with a brandy. Perhaps several. Who knows, if I drank enough of them I might even begin to understand the evening's events.

Holmes was quiet, clearly happy to listen to Silence's explanation and make his own conclusions. I had no doubt that those conclusions would likely be sceptical, and yet how could he doubt now? This wasn't the story of a single man, this was a series of incidents witnessed by a whole carriage – albeit bizarrely forgotten by most of them. One man lay dead, a victim of these infernal forces that seemed stacked against us. Surely even a man of logic, such as Holmes, must accept what was going on?

The door to our compartment opened and Carnacki stepped

inside, now wearing a shirt and smoking jacket.

Holmes took that moment to stand up, open the window and knock the bowl of his pipe against the frame, tipping the burned embers into the darkness below.

"These are murky waters," he admitted, "and I must confess I begin to wonder what use a man of reason may be amongst them. I am used to confronting the physical, the well-practiced criminal, the murderer, the thief... I have no experience of devils other than those metaphorical examples who lie behind the bars of our nation's gaols. Is this something that is beyond my scope?"

"Logic and scepticism are not out of place in the world of the supernatural detective," said Carnacki, sitting down and removing a cigar from a silver case in his pocket, "in fact I would consider them two of the most important weapons in my armoury. There are many times when I have been consulted on a case – or have taken it upon myself to investigate – only to find a perfectly rational explanation for the reported phenomena. I have thwarted imaginative smugglers, attempting to divert attention away from their store by perpetuating a belief in the 'Lost Sailor of Lulworth'. I have scotched the plans of no less than three impatient offspring seeking to encourage their parents into an early grave by scaring them to death. I am the man who put paid to the reputation of Stephen Jones, the so-called 'Wembley Horror', a man who claimed to channel some of the most infamous spirits of our age."

Silence pricked up his ears at that, though I must admit the reference meant little to me. "That was you, was it?" he asked Carnacki.

The younger man nodded. "He was merely seeking publicity for a new compendium of supernatural investigations he had edited. He channelled little but his ill-gotten gains into whisky."

Holmes had refilled his pipe and proceeded to smoke it, a common, if unhealthy, replacement for his forgoing an evening meal.

"Very well," he said, "so there is still a place for deduction and reason. Perhaps, from what you say, more so than in many of my cases, for mine can be the voice that leads us away from a natural inclination towards the supernatural."

"I fail to see how else this evening's events could be explained," I said, almost with regret.

Holmes shrugged. "It would seem to defy any rational explanation." He looked to Carnacki. "How did you become involved in these matters?" he asked.

"As you may have gathered my workload is fairly evenly divided between phenomena I choose to investigate and those I am hired to investigate. This was one of the latter, though regretfully I can tell you little about the man who hired me. He went absurdly out of his way to ensure that his identity remained secret."

"Why would someone do that I wonder?" asked Holmes.

"It's not uncommon," Carnacki said, "I face a great deal of scepticism in my line of work —"

"You're not the only one," interrupted Silence, casting a slight smile towards Holmes.

Carnacki ignored him. "The people that ask for my involvement are often embarrassed to have done so, or fearful that others will get to hear that they've taken such unorthodox steps. My case files are littered with anonymous letters. What is intriguing about this case, however, is that I actually met the man face to face."

I was first contacted in the Reading Room of the British Museum where I had been reading up on acoustics in the hope of developing a machine with which to negate a banshee's cry. I am a great believer in the application of science and practical thinking when it comes to combating the supernatural.

I was gathering my papers, meaning to retire to a little place I know in Fitzrovia for a light lunch, when I noticed a small rectangle of black card.

"Do you still have this black card by any chance?" asked Holmes.

Carnacki shook his head. "Now... if you let me tell my story without interruptions?"

Holmes smiled and waved his hand for the younger man to continue.

The note requested my presence at the office of a small publishing house just off Great Russell Street, claiming that it concerned a matter of "intense mutual interest".

Well, gentlemen, I must confess I am easily swayed by the dramatic and, having already taken a break in my researches, I went straight to meet the appointment.

The office was hidden away in a particularly unloved alcove of Gilbert Place and claimed to be that of the foremost specialist publisher of occult literature in the country. A claim immediately disproved by the fact that I had never heard of it. I entered and rang the bell on the reception desk in order to gain someone's attention.

Presently a small gentlemen appeared from a rear office. What hair he lacked on his head was more than compensated by that which grew from his chin. In fact the beard was almost an encumbrance, wrapped as it was between the large pile of books he was carrying. When he placed the books on the desk it was with considerable care that he stood up, slowly withdrawing his curly hairs from between the covers of the dusty volumes.

"Can I help you sir?" he asked, in that awkward and croaky-voiced way of the true bibliophile, men who have lost all semblance of human contact between the library stacks. I gave him the card I had found and he ferreted within his beard for a light pair of pince-nez that hung from a chain and had become lost. Popping them onto the bridge of his nose, he scrutinised the card.

"Ah," he said, dropping the card into his pocket, "yes, I was warned to prepare for that. You will be Mr Thomas Carnacki?"

"I am and always will be," I replied. "You were expecting me then?"

"Indeed, sir." As an after thought he extended his hand. He then glanced down at it, noticed it was covered in dust, brushed it against his tatty waistcoat and extended it once more. I shook it, not wanting to be mean-spirited. "I'm Algernon Newman, proprietor, publisher, senior editor and art director here at New Man Publishing."

"And receptionist?" I couldn't help but ask.

He had the grace to simply smile. "Times being what they are it's frightfully difficult to find reliable, economical staff," he admitted, "especially when working at the more... specialised end of the publishing market."

"One can imagine." We seemed to be in real danger

of forgetting the purpose of my visit so I reminded him. "You said you were expecting me?"

"Indeed." Newman gestured for me to follow him behind the desk and out through the door he had just entered from. "One of our authors, a particularly knowledgeable fellow, wished to make your acquaintance," he explained. "There were, however, some unusual requirements that he wished us to assist him with."

"Really?"

"Oh yes," Newman said, "and we do so like to be of service to our authors."

The corridor we were walking down appeared to be becoming darker and darker the further we moved along it. Navigating the offices of New Man Publishing was an act similar to potholing, for all its apparent modesty, the place was labyrinthine, dark and treacherous underfoot.

"Oh do mind those," Newman said as I tripped over a small pile of fur-lined volumes, "they are bound in goat hide and quite slippery."

I managed to avoid asking why a book should be bound as if for cold weather. In truth, as a man who has frequently had to peruse the most bizarre esoteric volumes in the line of his work, goat's fur was one of the most wholesome binding materials I have come across.

He led me to a small room at the end of the corridor and opened the door onto pitch blackness. "Please sir," he said, "if you can tolerate the informality I would ask that you take my hand. I fear there is no other way to lead you safely."

I did as asked and was led, blind, into the room. I could see nothing of my surroundings though I could smell the dusty pages of old books and leather covers, a scent that had been omnipresent though it was much stronger here. Newman moved in a precise manner, like a man learning a complicated dance. I could hear him counting under his breath, so many steps forward, so many steps to the left, then so many to the right. It was quite the most bizarre experience.

"This is our most precious storeroom," Newman explained, "some of the volumes here are so ancient that the merest touch of sunlight on their pages would likely send them to dust."

"How then can you read them?" I asked.

Newman chuckled. "Nobody would want to read these books, sir," he replied, "they're far too dangerous."

He halted, turned and sat me down carefully in a small, wooden chair.

"If you could just stay there, sir," he said, "our author will be with you shortly. I would ask that you don't try and navigate the storeroom independently, I couldn't be held responsible for the accidents that would naturally occur."

With that, either a polite threat or a just another piece of nonsense, he retreated into the darkness and I was left to wait.

While I sat there I endeavoured to sense as much as possible from my surroundings. I have already mentioned the smell of old books, but there were other clues too. There was the smell of something green, a sweet, evergreen scent. After a few moments, being reminded pointedly of graveyards, I realised it was the smell of yew trees. The other smell was less natural: old copper, turned verdigris over time. The sharp smell of old garden ornaments, of public monuments in the rain. Quite what it could be doing in such an environment was beyond me. Though perhaps my senses were beginning to cheat as I could also swear to movement in the room, the sound of tiny feet, such as an animal might make in forest undergrowth, the snuffling of a creature on the scent of its next meal. Perhaps there were rats in the storeroom, I'm sure the proprietor would never have known. At one point I even felt a cool breeze on my cheeks, as if someone had opened a door or window to the outside, after a moment the air was gone and I was plunged once more into the heavy atmosphere of dusty books.

"Mr Carnacki?" a voice asked. I placed it as several feet ahead of me, far enough away to be muffled by the presence of an obstacle between us, likely bookshelves. "Thank you for agreeing to meet with me in such unconventional circumstances." The voice was not just muffled by the clutter of the room. The speaker was disguising the tone in some way, it had that hollowed-out quality of a voice channelled through a speaking trumpet.

"At the time I wasn't aware that the circumstances would be so unconventional," I replied, "though you've certainly caught my attention."

"That is good," said the voice, "as that is certainly our goal. Tell me," he continued, "what do you know of the Breath of God?"

"I believe it's mentioned in some of the more questionable apocrypha?" I replied. "A variation on the wrath of God. Some books claim it is a tornado made from the spirits of the dead. Not much, though," I admitted eventually. "It's a reference I'm familiar with, a theological curiosity."

"It is much more than that," said the voice, "it is a genuine phenomenon, a force that is on the brink of being released into this world."

Claims of this sort were unlikely to move me. After all, ancient evils poised to return were something of an occupational cliché. "Is that so?" I replied. "Well, I'm happy to look into it but I'm rather busy at the moment so I can't promise that..."

"Do please hush, Mr Carnacki," said the voice. "I wouldn't be talking to you unless matters were a good deal more definite than that. I know a great deal about you and would hardly be wasting my or your time on a vague possibility."

"For someone who claims to know a great deal about me," I replied tersely, "you appear ignorant of the fact that if there's one thing I hate, it's being interrupted."

"Apologies, but time is precious to both of us and I sought to save some of it."

"Very well," I said, "then please continue."

"You will no doubt have heard of the Hermetic Order of the Golden Dawn." The voice was so confident of the fact – and rightly so – that it didn't give me time to reply. "There are certain forces within that organisation that are determined not only to break away from the main body of membership, but also to bring about changes to our society that would be disastrous. It has always been an unfortunate truth that people, when faced with the potential for power, often lose what altruistic intentions they may previously have had in order to fulfil their own selfish ambitions. This is the case here, and while a number of powerful and influential members are determined to stop them, this breakaway group is close to fulfilling their lunatic goal. They will let nothing stand in their way, Mr Carnacki, nothing and no one. You will have heard of the death of Hilary De Montfort?"

"Indeed."

"That is their first strike, it will not be their last. They seek to kill every member who opposes them, until there is nobody left with the skills to stop them."

"And what has this to do with me?"

"I cannot be seen to act, I wish to employ you as my agent in the matter. If your reputation is even half-earned, you have the skills and tenacity that may yet see this situation nipped in the bud."

"I can assure you my reputation is wholly earned. However, yours is nonexistent and yet you're asking me to place rather a lot of trust in you."

"I'm asking you nothing of the sort. You can't take the risk that I'm wrong and once you begin investigating I have every faith that you will learn enough to convince you. I need give you only three names: Lord Ruthvney, Sherlock Holmes and Aleister Crowley. From there you're on your own."

With that, the sensation of cool air returned, this time I could have sworn it brought with it the scent of the ocean, that hint of salt and seaweed. When it vanished again, leaving me with that ever-present stench of ageing paper, I knew that the speaker had gone. You will notice that I do not say I was left alone because that would have been far from the truth. I had sensed creatures in the darkness before, you will remember that I described the sound of their feet, the snuffling of their breath as they picked out scents amongst the shelves. They seemed to return in quantity now as a noise that I had first thought to be trickling water clarified itself as the scurry of hundreds of tiny feet.

"Newman?" I shouted. "Newman!"

There was no reply and I decided that I was damned if I was going to sit and wait, and perhaps be a generous supper for the rats, or whatever they might be.

I got to my feet and deciding not to strike a match for fear of what the light might attract, tried to remember the direction in which I had first been led. Slowly, shuffling my feet rather than taking large steps, I began to work my way back the way I felt I had come. It was only a few moments before I came into direct collision with a bookcase. Cursing, I held out my hands and felt my way along it, moving quicker while I had the wooden shelves to guide me. Even then there were piles of books on the floor and frequently I sent them crashing, slipping and tripping over them as I tried to work my way past.

I continued to call for Newman as I walked, undecided as to whether he was deaf or seeking to make life unpleasant for me. He had seemed pleasant enough but the whole business had soured so far that I was no longer inclined to give anyone the benefit of the doubt. It was a contradiction, if these people wanted me to investigate matters then why were they acting as if they themselves were the aggressors? It takes more than the dark to scare me, however, and I continued to make my way as quickly and safely as I could.

It was not just rats that moved in that darkness. I heard something running between the rows. It had bare feet, there was a slapping on the stone floor that could only come from skin rather than shoe leather. I had been calling for Newman, even though I was now quite convinced he would not respond. Still the sound had helped to guide me as I judged the way it bounced back at me from the far wall that must contain the door I had entered by. Now I no longer wished to draw such attention to myself.

I moved as silently as I could, keeping close to the book cases, feeling my way along them in the direction I felt sure led to the exit.

Whatever else that shared that storeroom with me seemed to have much less problem seeing, or certainly it had less fear of hurting itself as it ran up and down the rows. Sometimes it sounded like it might be climbing the shelves, as I heard its percussive grunts rising and the toppling of books spilled by its naked feet as it scaled towards the roof. What could it want in there but me? But why would these people unleash something dangerous on me? If they had wanted me dead then surely they had

had ample opportunity to kill me. But perhaps this was not the work of Newman or his secretive author, perhaps this was a foot soldier for the opposition, a creature of those darker forces within the Golden Dawn. Perhaps my faceless informant lay somewhere here, amongst the pages of these forgotten volumes, dead because he had dared to take a stand against them.

These were the thoughts that followed me as I made my way towards the door and the freedom that I hoped lay beyond it.

Behind me the creature was drawing closer. Its breathing sharp but regular as it ran faster and faster towards me. I could tell from the way the noise was dampened and muted then loud and echoing that it was zigzagging up and down the rows. Why it should take such a circuitous route was beyond me. Perhaps, rather than simply running directly to me it wanted to scare me first, build up the tension, force me to crack... It was close to succeeding. *Slap, slap, slap* came its feet on the concrete floor, ever louder with each passing second. I pride myself on being a man of considerable nerve and yet being cut off like this, disorientated by the loss of one sense and the resultant heightening of the others, I was close to breaking. It was all I could do not to run, panicked, into the darkness.

Nonetheless I moved as fast I could, taking long, careful strides until – with almost a cry of relief – I found myself at the far wall. My hands touched the cool plaster and skimmed along it, hoping to meet the door frame. Behind me the feet cleared the end of a row of shelves, the noise echoing around the end of the storeroom. My fingers met the edge of the door frame just as I became aware that the creature behind me was not re-entering the row of bookshelves, rather it was running straight towards me.

I snatched for the door handle as the sound of its bare feet grew so close I could hardly believe it hadn't reached me.

It only occurred to me to worry about the door being locked a fraction of a second before I opened it, stepped through and slammed it shut behind me. The weight of the creature hit the solid wood and nearly rebounded me from it. I grabbed the handle and threw my weight back, holding the door closed even as the creature continued to pound against it from the other side. My hands were sweating and threatened to slip from the handle.

I was just preparing for the fact that soon it would manage to tear the door from my weak grip when finally it gave up. Pressing my ear to the wood I could just hear its naked feet running away from the door, retreating deeper into the storeroom.

Perhaps it knew of another way out?

I ran along the narrow corridor between the storeroom and the front office, frequently checking over my shoulder in case the creature had doubled back and was now on my tail. As I reached the door to the office I came crashing to a halt. Something was pushed against it from the other side, keeping it closed. I dropped my shoulder to the wood and charged at it, sending the heavy weight on the other

side sliding along a few inches with every shove. Soon the space was wide enough for me to slip past. I clambered around the jamb of the door and stumbled into the front office, toppling over the weight that had kept the door closed. It was the body of Algernon Newman.

I moved to check his pulse, though it was clear from his terrified face that he was dead and had not gained the condition comfortably. As I pressed against the small man's body it made the most hideous crinkling noise. His stomach, bloated beyond its previous condition, sank beneath my fingers with the slow, crumpled sound of a cheap mattress. From Newman's lips a couple of compressed pieces of paper tumbled: pages, torn from books, screwed up and then forced past that absurd beard and into the poor man's mouth. He was full of paper, fit to burst with the pages from his own precious books.

Disgusted, I got to my feet and ran from that man's offices, back into the cool air of a Bloomsbury afternoon.

CHAPTER FOURTEEN

Emergency Stop

I need hardly say that Carnacki's tale had captured all our attentions. Even Holmes, a man not disposed towards the pleasures of an eerie tale told by firelight, had listened intently after his initial, aggressively rebutted, interruption. Of course, in Holmes' case, I had little doubt that his analytical mind had been attempting to explain away every apparently supernatural element to Carnacki's story, beating each and every moment of terror with a stick of logic. Perhaps he was right to do so. Certainly, before tonight, I would have done the same.

Now, however, my faith in the logical and rational had been almost entirely stripped away. I no longer knew what I could believe in, and I can honestly say that that, in itself, was one of the most terrible experiences of my life. We are quite unaware how much we rely on our fragile prisons of belief, whether those prisons are forged of Gods, science, or elements of both, they are what protect us and they are also the filter through which we experience life. We read a tragic story in the newspaper, we see a child die, we hear the sabre-rattling of war... all these things are factored and related to via our beliefs. And without that simple structure, that rigidity, that arrogant assumption that we understand the world and our place in it... well, without that, we are utterly exposed.

"Of course," said Carnacki, "once I was back beneath the hazy sun of a London afternoon I began to wonder just what it had all meant. It seemed to me that a great deal of effort had gone into unnerving me. In itself this was not unusual in matters where the supernatural plays a hand. In fact, as you are no doubt aware, Dr Silence, many manifestations of a supernatural nature rely on the fear they create in others in order to survive. It is that mental energy that makes them strong. Still, I wondered what the purpose of it all had been, and whether my mysterious informant was victim or perpetrator.

"Settling my nerves with a brandy in the Fitzroy Tavern just off Great Russell Street, I came to the conclusion that, whatever the ultimate intent behind that afternoon's horror show, I had little choice but to make an investigation into the small amount that I had been told. I made an anonymous phone call to the police to inform them of Newman's demise (having no wish to find myself sat in front of an interview desk all afternoon) and returned to the British Museum in order to make some more notes on the so-called Breath of God. I didn't learn a great deal more than I had already known, it seemed to me to be a general catch-all for those more imaginative religious authors wanting to put the shivers into their readers.

"We are all only too familiar, I am sure, of the distinct shift in holy attitude throughout the books of the Bible. God grows from being a vengeful, almost sadistic creature, to one of beneficence with an almost infinite capacity for forgiveness. The Breath of God seemed to me to be a creation distinctly intended to bring to mind the terrifying patriarch of the former attitude. An invisible force unleashed upon God's enemies and capable of the most terrible destruction imaginable. These theologians do so like to keep their audience scared."

"Fear keeps the churches full," agreed Silence.

"And, with respect, keeps you employed," added Holmes. "If people weren't scared of the darker potential of the spirit, they would hardly be in need of your services, would they?"

Neither Silence nor Carnacki deigned to reply.

Carnacki continued his story as if Holmes had not spoken: "But then if the Breath of God is was what killed De Montfort then clearly it was not something to be taken lightly. And from examining the medical report it would seem that the police are at a loss for a more conventional explanation."

"How on earth did you get to read that?" I asked.

"Oh," Carnacki replied, "the surgeon, Cuthbert Wells, is a friend of mine."

I glanced at Holmes who merely smiled.

"In fact it was Wells that put me in touch with a young Inspector Mann who I believe you met recently?"

"Indeed we did," I said. "Holmes was good enough to help him with the investigation into Lord Ruthvney's death."

Carnacki nodded. "As was I. Though I'll warrant that the inspector has precious little his superiors will tolerate his putting in a report."

"Then perhaps you were not as much help as he might have hoped?" I replied, realising even as I said it that I sounded childishly defensive.

Carnacki shrugged. "I cannot change the facts, that Ruthvney was killed by forces outside the normal purview of the police force should have been self-evident to anyone with a modicum of intelligence."

"That would rather depend on your point of view," said Holmes. "If you were of a decidedly rational bent then you would of course discount the application of supernatural forces as impossible and therefore still strive to find another solution."

"You can't still be sceptical?" Silence asked. "After everything we've experienced!"

"Thus far I have experienced nothing," Holmes replied, "but I've heard a great deal. Gentlemen, if you will excuse me I really must see about dinner, this realist mind of mine will insist on sustenance. Perhaps you would be happy to keep me company?" he asked me. Of course I agreed and we left, a somewhat uncomfortable silence following us out into the train corridor.

"I think I feel a Baskerville manoeuvre coming, Watson," said Holmes once we had sat down in the dining carriage. "Which is why I forced you to accompany me, we must have a words in private."

I felt deeply uncomfortable sat there, staring in a daze towards the ceiling where that terrifying web had hung. The unfortunate gentleman who had not survived the experience had of course been moved now, no doubt laid down in an empty carriage to await the police at the next station. They would not be happy to see the body moved but with an official assurance from Silence that the man had died of natural causes – something I had no doubt he would give, the alternative being impossible to prove – no doubt the law would be content. I only wished it was so easy for me. Looking back now I realise I was in a state of shock, my mind slipping from minutiae to daydream, fixating on anything it could lay its hands on rather than face what it was unable to process. At the time I just felt dreadfully tired, confused and barely able to keep up with Holmes' conversation.

"A Baskerville manoeuvre?" I asked.

"I cannot stay here, my friend," he said, selecting an escalope of veal from the menu and a bottle of claret which he no doubt assumed we would share.

I began to protest but he held up his hand.

"Forgive me," he said, "but I cannot. The position is untenable. I cannot work with them any more than they could work with me. We are too opposed in our beliefs."

"If you had only seen what we saw..."

"But I did not, and therefore I cannot believe it."

"You could take me at my word."

"My dear fellow," he insisted, "there's nobody's word I value more. But even taking that into account, all I can say for sure is that *you* believe it happened. That is not the same thing as *my* believing it happened."

"Short of a demon leaping out of your soup and grabbing you by the necktie, I doubt anything could convince you."

"Precisely my point. But until that happens, can we agree that I respect you enormously but that I am a cold fish that insists on empirical evidence before he'll so much as listen to another ghost story?"

I smiled. However much I may have wished for my friend to be the one who could share and explain these things to me, he would hardly have been Sherlock Holmes had he done so. "Agreed," I said. "In truth I don't know what to think myself, but what I saw..."

"Is what you saw," he said, "and was either real or not. My only advice – and it is meant kindly – is that you question everything but, for the sake of your sanity, be *willing* to believe. I know you may think that I am utterly rigid in my outlook but in truth I could be convinced. The science of today is the magic of yesterday, who's to say what impossibilities may become commonplace in the future? But big claims require big evidence and thus far I have yet to see enough to change my view of the world."

"Very well," I agreed. "I shall continue to observe objectively and, so far as I can, rationally. What are you going to do?"

"Oh, you know me," he said with a smile, "I shall follow my own lines of enquiry. Ah! The veal..."

Sometimes I could almost swear that Holmes had the entire serving community in his employ, the amount of times an explanation has been diverted by a dinner plate beggars belief. He sniffed the dish and smiled a smile of pure, innocent pleasure.

Many considered Holmes a cold and humourless man, for which I suppose I must take the blame. If my writing has made him seem so then I have done him a disservice. He could be obsessive, insensitive and unfeeling but I would never say these were his default emotions. He simply wasn't very good with people – over the years I like to think I became an exception – and he often tended to repel them with harsh words rather than go through the troublesome business of having to interact with them. Yet even that is misleading, however, now I read it back, for Holmes could also be exceptionally charming, particularly with women – which would surprise a number of his commentators I'm sure. Perhaps the key to Holmes' character lies in his contradictions rather than his consistencies. When in a cheerful mood he could be electric, his humour and charm second to none. When at a lower ebb he could be quite intolerable, even cruel. Holmes was, quite simply, a fractured man. But then what genius can claim to be stable?

"I take it you wish me to keep in touch?" I said, helping myself to a glass of the wine as he began to eat.

"Most definitely," he agreed. "As usual, simply send all correspondence to Baker Street and I shall have it rerouted from there."

"To little more than a stone's throw away, I imagine."

"I will certainly keep a close eye, but this case has its feelers spread wide, I will need to travel here and there in the hope of bringing it to some semblance of order."

"And what shall I tell the others?"

Holmes thought about that for a moment. "That is certainly important," he said, "I would not want them to think I have abandoned matters. Tell them..." He continued to think, a piece of veal hovering on his fork, then he gave a contented smile. "Tell them that the De Montfort family have been applying pressure and that my brother has demanded an audience. Tell them that I shall placate him as swiftly as possible, reassure him that all is in hand, and then return."

I agreed that I would say just that.

Finishing his meal, Holmes checked his watch. "I dare say our ghostly sleuths will be getting impatient. You should return to the fold and make my excuses."

"And where will you go? They can't help but notice that we're on a moving train, you can hardly have vanished."

"Can't I? I would have thought that would have been well within their widened realms of possibility." He stood up, reached for the emergency stop chain and yanked it.

"Oh Holmes..." I said as the carriage filled with the sound of brakes and passengers erupted in a panic.

"See you soon," said Holmes, running from the carriage with a childlike chuckle.

I made my way back to the carriage we had been sharing with Dr Silence and Carnacki.

As I came in sight of it along the train corridor, Carnacki stuck his head out of the door. "What's happening?" he asked.

"Holmes," I replied, not for the first time using my friend's name as an explanation for chaos. "He's received an urgent wire from his brother, Mycroft."

I entered the carriage and sat back down, glancing at my friend's overnight case in the rack and realising that I would now be forced to carry it along with my own. "It seems the De Montfort family are dissatisfied with the progress of the investigation thus far," I said, "and have put pressure on him through their connections in government. Holmes' brother has been tasked with consoling them."

"A thankless undertaking one imagines," said Silence. "Given the facts of the case."

"Nonetheless, Mycroft has insisted that Holmes returns to London immediately in order to show that everything possible is being done. He is adamant that he will rejoin us as soon as he can."

"Perhaps it's for the best," said Carnacki. "I appreciate from your stories that he is a talented detective, Dr Watson, but, given my involvement, that is not a skill that we are currently lacking. His scepticism was an unnecessary hurdle that we now have no need to jump."

"I can assure you that his presence could only have been an asset," I said, defensively, "and I have no doubt he will return shortly."

"Well," said Silence, "*I* certainly hope so, given that the spirits asked for him directly, I can't say I relish he fact that he's no longer with us."

"Relax," said Carnacki, "the spirits will just have to be content with me!"

CHAPTER FIFTEEN

Assassin in the Night

As the train continued north, Carnacki filled the time with more stories of his exploits. For all his arrogance he told a good tale and I confess I enjoyed listening to him. The thrill of his adventures only slightly marred once it occurred to me that, if all he was saying was true – something I could no no longer entirely dismiss – then our current experiences were far from isolated incidents. Carnacki had, as previously admitted, been involved in several cases where the supernatural had not been involved, rather the evil hands of man wishing to convince otherwise. Accepting that, there was still the matter of the disembodied tongue that wagged within the dining room of Brackridge Hall or the squealing of the Pig Lords that had so terrified those in residence at Mocata Grange.

The world in which both Silence and Carnacki operated was not the world in which I had hitherto lived. The safe, solid world I was used to seemed little more than a stepping stone to other existences and experiences. I tried to bear Holmes' advice in mind, to listen, and be willing to believe, but to also accept that their tales may have grown in the telling, that perhaps the gelatinous spectre of Andover Crescent was the result of misunderstood evidence, events that could have had an explanation through science as well as the supernatural.

I was still deeply unsettled, however, and even when I began to feel tiredness sweeping over me I found I couldn't close my eyes against the furniture of the carriage. In my mind's eye I found it all too easy to imagine faces appearing in the darkness of the window, the light of the lamps dimming, hands moving beneath the upholstery of the seats. I had lost all faith in the comfort of my surroundings.

Accordingly, when we finally approached Inverness, I was exhausted and agitated. Desperate for sleep but unable to give in to it.

The train pulled up and we descended with our luggage. I placed both mine and Holmes' bags on the platform and checked my watch. It was just shy of midnight. Our plan had been to find a hotel close to the station so that we might sleep and recommence our journey towards Foyers, where Boleskine House lay, in the morning. At this time of night we certainly didn't fancy doing much more than securing a bed.

"I dare say there's a railway hotel nearby," said Silence. "What say I check with one of the porters?"

He walked over to a short, red-faced man who was wrestling with the hatboxes of the elderly lady I had been saddled with earlier. They talked for a few moments, and then Silence returned.

"There's a place not five minutes walk away," he announced, "and apparently what they lack in refined decoration they more than make up for with breakfast."

"I'm sure I'll have stayed in worse," said Carnacki, picking up his bag and following Silence towards the exit. I went to pick up my own bags and suddenly realised that Holmes' case had vanished. It had been no more than a foot from mine but now it was gone. I looked around, about to raise a cry of alarm when it occurred to me that the only person who could have stolen it with such skill and subtlety was probably its owner, and that maybe Holmes hadn't left the train earlier at all.

"Infuriating man," I muttered to myself, chasing to catch up with Silence and Carnacki.

At the entrance to the station we were directed up the street a short distance to the doors of Unsworth Lodge, bed and breakfast. Despite concerns of the late hour, the door was answered almost immediately by a small lady who had that mothball air of a woman caught in the hinterland of middle-age. Her hair was striped in black and white like that of a badger and her mouth was perpetually puckered as if she were in the process of devouring an everlasting pickled onion.

"Mr Holmes and company?" she asked, before we had even had a chance to speak.

"Actually," I said, "Mr Holmes is not with us but I am Dr Watson and these are my colleagues, Dr Silence and Mr Thomas Carnacki. Were you expecting us then?" I was unaware that Holmes had called ahead and booked us rooms, but supposed it was far from impossible.

"I most certainly was," the woman said, beckoning us in. "I can assure you I don't wait up at this hour on the off chance of custom." She looked at Carnacki. "Though you weren't on the booking, young man," she said to him before turning back to me. "Will Mr Holmes be arriving later?"

"Sadly not," I replied, "our plans had to change at the last minute."

She nodded as if this were all too common here at Unsworth Lodge. "Then I suppose he can have the spare room," she said, nodding towards Carnacki, "after all, I've cleaned and aired it now, it would be a great irritation were it not to be used."

"That would be excellent," I said and we followed her up a narrow flight of steps towards a landing that contained several numbered rooms.

She opened the doors marked three, five and seven and ushered us to take our pick. "There's no real difference," she said, "except for the noise of the rats in five. It's right beneath the loft you see and they've made themselves right at home up there."

Silence, who had been entering the door of the said room as she spoke, gave a slight sigh before carrying on. "Good night gentlemen," he said. "I trust I shall survive the night and see you in time for breakfast."

He pulled the door closed behind him and I said my goodbyes to Carnacki before entering my own room, number three. It occurred to me just before shutting the door, that I should ask the landlady something. "Excuse me," I said, calling her back from the stairs, "I know this might sound ridiculous but who was it that booked the rooms?"

She gave me a sharp look that said, yes, it certainly was a ridiculous thing to ask. "I would have thought you'd have known that yourselves," she said. "It was Mr Crowley, of course."

I was no more relaxed in my bedroom than I had been in the train carriage. How could Crowley have known? Had Holmes telegrammed ahead, or Silence even? Then Holmes' advice returned to me and, rather than get carried away with the possibility of unnerving conclusions, I accepted that the only way that Crowley could have known is that one or the other had told him. It scarcely mattered which, though it would have been nice to have been told, naturally...

I dressed for bed. It can't have been Silence, I thought, I had seen him ask the porter whether there was a hotel close by, he would hardly have done that if he had already known the answer... So it was Holmes then, I told myself, losing patience with my own inclination to question, and, as usual, he had chosen to keep it to himself as he never met a theatrical flourish he didn't love.

I turned down the gas and shuffled towards the bed, distracted for a moment by the sight of the moonlit street beyond the window. I stood between the curtains and looked out at the row of terraced houses. It took a few moments for my eyes to adjust, the moon was large and the clouds parted enough to let its light fall down on the quiet street. Looking on those rows of ordinary houses, I wondered what their, no doubt sleeping, residents might make of the night's events. Were they like me, rigid enough in their beliefs that any upset left them reeling? Or were they more superstitious, more willing to believe anything of the world they lived in?

I was about to turn away when I noticed the silhouette of a figure at the top of the street. I couldn't help but smile at that paper-thin shape in its top hat, swinging a cane as he walked away from me. I was certain I knew its owner and went to my bed feeling somewhat more secure for knowing that Holmes was still near by.

The good feeling didn't last and I awoke several times in the night. The first occasion was upon being shaken free of a terrible dream, a nightmare where viscous liquid had covered my face and body, forcing its tendrils up my nostrils and into my mouth. I had been hanging,

I remembered, as the cool air chilled the night sweats on my back, swinging in that ectoplasmic cat's cradle in the dining carriage, utterly at the mercy of whatever force it was that had hovered above us.

Lying there in the dark I tried to shake the feeling that I was not alone in my room, dismissing the unfamiliar silhouettes of the furniture around me as source for panic. The sound of breathing I thought I could hear was no doubt my own, echoed back at me from against the high ceiling, the delay making it sound like the breathing of another. I held my breath, finally sighing into the silence that resulted. The house creaked around me, of course, all houses do. I reminded myself also of the rats that our landlady insisted were thriving in the loft space above us. No doubt they made that tapping noise that, for one terrified second, I imagined was the sound of a nail on my door.

Finally, such childish thoughts ceased and I returned to sleep, only to be woken again some time later. Something had disturbed me, though I could not tell what. What I could hear, extremely faintly, was the sound of a man crying. I lit a match and checked my watch, it was a quarter to three in the morning. What is it that so saddened a man that it brought tears at this hour? Lying back in the darkness, the sharp smell of the match settling around me, I thought about my poor Mary and had my answer.

I woke early, with the beginnings of dawn breaking through a gap in the curtains and landing on the bed. It was an unhealthy, grey light and the sight of it brought me no pleasure or anticipation for the day ahead. I put on my slippers and went in search of hot water.

The landlady was stood in the middle of her kitchen, staring into space as if utterly empty of character. I imagined her having stood

that way all night, awaiting orders to bring her once more back to life. Her deep thoughts were interrupted by the sound of my feet on a creaking floorboard and she snapped to attention, giving me a somewhat unfriendly look and returning to her morning tasks.

"I wondered if I might have some hot water?" I asked, feeling, quite ridiculously, that such a thing was an imposition.

She nodded. "I'll bring some up to you, sir," she said. "Will you and your companions be wanting breakfast?"

"I imagine so," I replied. Then, self-consciously feeling I had to justify why I was making such demands at the early hour. "We have a lot planned for the day so an early start is always good."

"Been awake hours," she said, "a woman's work is never done."

"No," I responded, awkwardly. "I imagine not."

We both stood there for a few moments of uncomfortable silence. Then finally I decided one of us had to take the initiative or I'd never get back to my room. "Shall I take the water back up with me?" I asked. "It's no trouble."

"I said I'd bring it up," she replied, "and so I will." She set about filling a large pan from the tap over the sink and, feeling I'd been dismissed, I returned to my room and sat on the bed to wait. I could hear sounds of movement from next door and concluded that Silence was also awake. I thought about knocking on his door but was distracted by the arrival of the hot water.

I washed cautiously over the basin and dried myself off quickly, it was far too cold to linger.

Finally, dressed and feeling I had thoroughly scrubbed away the day and night before, I left my room and went to check on the others. Silence was, indeed, awake though by the look of him only barely. Perhaps he was like Holmes in that he was not a morning person.

I have my years in the army to thank for the fact that, once my eyes open, I am invariably as sharp as a tack. I arranged to meet Silence downstairs for breakfast in three-quarters of an hour.

There was no reply from Carnacki's room so I went downstairs to check with the landlady that breakfast would be convenient for the time I had arranged and then left the building, meaning to get a little morning air and a sense of my surroundings.

I have spoken of my love of London and, certainly, that is undiminished. The crispness of the Scottish air was most refreshing, however, a sharp and fresh taste in my mouth as I strode forth from the guesthouse and along the road towards the station.

Inverness was in its stride already, the shop doors open and the delivery boys racing to and fro on their bicycles. In the distance I could see the signs of a street market filling out and I considered visiting it before settling for something a little more peaceful and heading away from the centre towards the river. The red brick of Inverness Castle gleamed in that early morning light and, as I walked along the banks of the Ness, getting my thoughts in order and imagining what may lie ahead, I began to feel as content as I can remember. I would face whatever the day might bring, and I would do so with conviction and strength, however shocking it might be. Whatever lay ahead my restless night had convinced me of one thing: I had already faced the worst thing in life a man can bear, the death of someone he loves. Whatever else may come along it certainly wouldn't be as painful as that.

I picked up a newspaper on my return to the guesthouse, glancing through the main articles as I checked Carnacki's room once again (still no sign of the man) and then took a seat in the dining room to wait for Silence. He arrived shortly after, looking fresher now that he had washed and dressed.

"I hope you at least slept well, Doctor?" he asked.

"Actually," I replied, "I passed an abominable night, but hopefully the effects will soon pass with a decent breakfast inside me."

The landlady brought us a bowl of porridge each, thick as glue and salty to taste. I can't say I was enamoured of it and dearly hoped it would be a prelude to something better rather than a solitary course.

I told Silence about the night's revelation that our rooms had not been booked by Holmes as I had initially suspected but rather by Crowley himself. This was clearly news to him also, so I was left with the previous night's conclusion which I shared with Silence: Holmes must have wired Crowley in advance of our travelling and had matters arranged on our behalf. That would certainly explain why no provision had been made for Carnacki.

"Have you seen Carnacki this morning?" I asked Silence.

"No," he said, "I assumed he would be joining us shortly."

"Not unless he includes mind-reading in that not inconsiderable list of his abilities," I said. "I haven't been able to raise him."

SIlence looked concerned. "Do you think he's all right?"

"Having listened to him talk last night, I get the impression he's damn near impregnable. I imagine he is simply sleeping in and I don't intend to worry until after breakfast. That's as long as there is more to come."

Thankfully there was, bacon and eggs that wiped away the memory of the porridge after only a couple of mouthfuls.

It was as the landlady brought us a second pot of coffee that Carnacki appeared, looking as immaculate as ever.

"We started without you I'm afraid," I said, pouring him a cup of coffee.

"I breakfasted earlier," he announced, "the landlady was kind enough to give me the use of her kitchen for half an hour before the rest of the house awoke."

"Oh," I said, "up with the lark then?"

"I don't enjoy sleep," he replied, "it reminds me a little too much of death."

"A cheery thought to start the day," I commented.

"Here's another: during the night someone tried to kill me."

Both Silence and I were dumbfounded at this.

"I am extremely lucky," Carnacki continued, "that I enjoy a hard bed and found the offering of our charming landlady to be inadequate in that regard.

"After having retired from your company, I sat down to write some notes on the day's experiences," he held up a small, leather-bound journal. "I keep copious notes as one day I intend to compile a series of volumes covering the entirety of my professional career." He glanced in my direction. "For sure, if I don't tackle the job myself someone else will, and I would hate being at the mercy of a sloppy biographer.

"I had just begun establishing the details of the attack – and my remarkable defence – in the dining carriage when I heard the sound of someone moving around in the corridor outside our rooms. Initially I assumed it was the landlady, perhaps checking that we had turned off the gas, or whatever concerns parsimonious hosts in this part of the country. However, on closer attendance I could tell it was the footstep of a man, the tread was too heavy to be that of our landlady and there was the distinct creak of new shoe leather.

"I dropped to my knees by the door and looked out through the keyhole but, unsurprisingly, it was too dark to catch a glimpse of our late-night wanderer. I decided it was likely unimportant, it may simply have been one of the other guests, disturbed by our arrival."

"Are there any other guests?" I wondered, certainly none had as yet appeared for breakfast.

"Whoever it was," Carnacki continued, "they left the house and made their way up the street, I saw them from my window, but couldn't swear to any great detail, they were wearing a top hat and carrying a cane. That's all I could say for sure."

It occurred to me that I had seen the same figure and that Carnacki had likely mistaken Holmes for his mysterious intruder. Which, from Carnacki's point of view, I suppose he was.

"Returning to my notes, I wrote for maybe another half an hour or so and then arranged a pair of blankets and the pillow on the floor. The bed was between myself and the door, a fact I would later be grateful for.

"I was woken at around three by the noise of footsteps once again outside my room. There was a scraping noise at the lock as whoever it was outside attempted to pick it. It was no difficult task, I had inspected the locks when retiring and considered them barely sufficient for the name. My would-be assassin certainly made a meal of it, however. They may be comfortable with the crime of murder but they had certainly never tried breaking and entering before. After a couple of minutes I nearly got up to let them in, better that than lie there listening to their ineptitude.

"Thankfully I was saved that embarrassment by their finally rolling back the tumblers and gaining access. The door opened slowly and quietly. As there was no light in the corridor outside I was unable to discern the shape of the intruder. My curtains were drawn tight and there was no moonlight to help in either my recognition of the stranger or their desire to assassinate me. I heard the man's feet come a few steps into the room, then I heard him tap the edge of the bed with his foot. There was a dull noise, a hoarse cough, and the man retreated instantly, closing the door behind him. I gave it a few moments, just in case he had yet to leave, but I heard the sound of another door in the hall open and then close and I guessed that he had entered one of the other rooms. Obviously, the man was a resident like ourselves.

"I lit a candle and examined the bed. It was showered with feathers and there was a small hole top centre. The unknown assailant had fired a small calibre bullet at where he imagined my head to be, using a pillow folded around the muzzle of the gun as a method of silencing the shot. Further investigation revealed that he had dropped the pillow outside my door. I was tempted to knock on every door and have a confrontation there and then on the landing but, giving it some thought, I decided I would have no end of difficulty proving who the assailant was and little was to be gained from my alerting them immediately as to their failure. If nothing else it allowed me to conclude my sleep in peace."

"But," I said, "this is incredible, who would want you killed?"

"Ah," Carnacki replied, "that's where things get even more complicated. I'm rather afraid a man like me is no stranger to enemies. It could be something to do with this current case, but equally it could be an ancient grudge. There are a number of fellows who might wish to see me dead."

Can't think why, I thought to myself. Choosing to be more tactful aloud, I said: "We must be grateful they didn't succeed."

"Indeed," agreed Silence.

The sound of the doorbell rang throughout the lower floor and I watched our landlady shuffle towards the front door in clear irritation. She was not cut out for this job, I decided. If people irritate you as much as they clearly did her, you are best avoiding them entirely.

"Yes?" she asked of whoever was at the door.

The reply, given in a voice much quieter than her angry bark, wasn't heard. Though we were to know soon enough as she showed the man into the dining room.

"Your carriage is here, sirs," she said. "Now mind I haven't been paid for these rooms before you go dashing off."

I asked her how much we owed her for her charming company and rooms and we settled our bills accordingly.

On the doorstep stood a thin, cheerful-looking fellow by the name of Charles. "Here to drive you to Boleskine," he said. "Want a hand with your bags?"

"Just a couple of minutes to go and grab them," I replied, as the others went to pack their things. "I'm afraid we weren't informed that you would be coming."

"Aye," said Charles, "that sounds like the boss right enough, always got his head in the clouds that one." It suddenly occurred to him that maybe he was speaking out of turn, a worried look passing over his face. "In a manner of speaking at least," he said, "I mean no ill by it."

I gave him a smile and patted him reassuringly on the arm. "Don't worry," I said, "speak as freely as you like, I don't know the man from Adam." I had been hoping, as I'd often seen Holmes do in similar circumstances, that this attempt to befriend the man would lead to a few more revelations about Crowley. I was to be disappointed. Charles seemed genuinely worried that he may have offended his employer and was far too concerned to utter another word. Cursing what I took to be my own ham-fisted attempts at winning the fellow over I went to collect my own belongings.

CHAPTER SIXTEEN

THE LAIRD OF BOLESKINE

Soon we were on the road out of Inverness and commencing what would be an interminably long ride along the shores of Loch Ness towards the village of Foyers.

I suppose, had the mood been different, then I would have found the Loch a beautiful place. On that drive, however, I found its flat grey waters a dismal sight. The weather was gloomy, rain attempting to wash away the thick snow, and it lent everything a feeling of oppression.

I watched a sparrowhawk ride a terrified finch through the damp air, its talons digging into the smaller bird's back as it surfed the currents, tiring out its prey. I am not normally sensitive to nature's cruelty but that day it left a sour taste, and I stopped looking out of the window.

My travelling companions seemed no less affected by the atmosphere. Silence lived up to his name, while Carnacki seemed ensconced in reading his notes of investigations past. None of us attempted to strike up a conversation and, for perhaps the first time, it became clear that all three of us travelled together through convenience rather than desire. We didn't know each other, nor did we have any great wish to. We were always destined to be polite strangers.

I took the time offered to write to Holmes, detailing all that happened since we had parted company the night before, including as much detail as I could, knowing how he always loved hearing all the minutiae. It was no easy task in the shaking carriage but I decided I didn't need to apologise in the letter for my appalling handwriting, certainly Holmes would have decided the manner in which it had been written before he got past the envelope.

Eventually, after nearly three hours of the carriage being buffeted by the poor road surface and the inhospitable wind, we went through a grand archway. Riding past a small, stone gatehouse, the track led us up above the road. We passed another building – a separate guest house, I would later discover, called Brown Lodge – and, more alarmingly, a graveyard. "He keeps cheerful company," I joked.

As the house came into view I confess I was momentarily taken aback by how grand it was. Two double-storied buildings stood on either side of the entrance courtyard, a single-storied building connecting them and completing the angular C shape. Its owner would insist on referring to it as a manor house, a phrase which did nothing to convey its grandiosity. But then, the same could be said of its owner. Crowley was never anything less than the consummate publicist and in the years that would follow he would become famous even outside those occult circles in which he moved, feared and admired in almost equal measure by a populace that would one day relish in calling him "the wickedest man in the world".

"Gentlemen!" called a voice from the main entrance and I took a moment to appreciate my first sight of the man who would go on to such notoriety. It was a light voice, and his was a soft, young face. Dressed in full Highland dress, Aleister Crowley was not the man I had imagined him to be, and in that perhaps I hit on something that would be a constant in his life. Most frequently through the creation of a public persona almost entirely at odds with reality, Aleister Crowley would *forever* be other than what you might imagine.

Today he was a man of great geniality, striding out into the rain to open the door to the carriage and welcome us down. "So glad you're finally here," he said, "you must be sorely in need of warmth and food, both of which I am happy to offer!"

He waved at a tall, thin man who I took to be his butler. "The bags please, McGillicuddy," he said, ushering us into the building ahead of him.

"Welcome, gentlemen," he said, "most welcome." A housekeeper bustled forth, taking our hats and coats while Crowley led us along a lengthy corridor that appeared to extend the entire length of the house. "If only there were a less damaging method of seeing you to my door," he said as we filed into a large reception room, massive fire blazing while the stuffed heads of big game looked on. I found myself reminded of Lord Ruthvney's office and the mental association put me even further on edge. "Hopefully you were at least recovered from the train journey thanks to the sour ministrations of Unsworth Guest House?" He laughed and waved for us to sit down, dropping into a leather armchair himself.

"It was most kind of you to arrange it, sir," I said, happy to speak on behalf of us all. "Though I confess we were a little taken aback that you were expecting us."

"Now," said Crowley with a smile, "what sort of practitioner of Magick would I be had I not been expecting you?"

I politely returned the smile. "I thought perhaps that my colleague, Mr Sherlock Holmes, had contacted you."

"I've never heard from him," said Crowley and, with a somewhat irritated tone I noted, he added, "what is more it appears that I never shall. I had hoped he would be with you."

"It is his intention to return as soon as he can," I explained, "but important business called him back to London."

"Ah yes," Crowley replied, "what it is to be at the mercy of 'important business.'"

"Perhaps he simply tired of our company," said Carnacki, "or felt the situation was beyond him." He got to his feet and extended his hand to Crowley for shaking. "Thomas Carnacki," he said, "a pleasure to make your acquaintance."

"I am only too aware who you are," Crowley assured him, shaking the hand.

"Really? How gratifying." Carnacki turned his back towards the fire, warming himself. "You're in terrible danger you know."

"An occupational hazard," Crowley replied.

"Please," Silence spoke at last, "you mustn't dismiss the threat you are under, from what we can tell it is of the highest order."

"I'm quite sure it is," Crowley responded, "and I am most grateful for your concern, but your warning – while kind – was unnecessary. Let us eat, then I shall make clear to you that I am quite aware of the danger I am in, after all, I have spent the last few days effectively under siege in my own home."

CHAPTER SEVENTEEN

INTERLUDE: THE ACCOUNT OF ALEISTER CROWLEY

I have not been a resident here for many months, I bought the house from the previous owner due to its suitability for a ritual I had in mind.

Life here could hardly be more different than it was during the last couple of years in London. You may know a little of my history but let me just say that, despite my age, my progression through the ranks of The Hermetic Order of the Golden Dawn has been astonishingly swift. I was initiated into their ranks only two years ago and yet I am now, through both my own researches and the tutelage of the great Arnold Bennett, considered one of the foremost adepts in the country. In truth, gentlemen, the Order is not all it might be and its reputation owes as much to its strict onus on secrecy as it does to the Magickal skills gathered there. Nothing seems so important as a locked room, does it? We cannot help but imagine all manner of exciting things go on there.

Perhaps this caused unrest amongst my fellow members. Certainly there were those who complained of the close friendship I shared with Arnold and made claims that we were betraying the trust of the Order and dabbling in matters with which we had no business. What can I say? For all its high-handed proclamations, the Order is as predictable a group of nonentities as might be expected when any group of people attempts to set itself up as exclusive. I bear them no ill will you understand, quite the reverse, but it has become clear that they could not say the same of me.

Since retiring from London I had sought a life of peace here overlooking the Loch, I am a person quite at home in the countryside, and wished no more than to be accepted within the bosom of the community. Something I am glad to say I have achieved, albeit with a few false starts... Remind me to let you taste some of the local liquor left for me as a bribe to silence! There is a local still nearby which lives in fear of the excise men...

I spend most of my days on or near the Loch, fishing for salmon or merely taking in the air, it has a charm and quality you'll not find in the smoky confines of London, sirs, I assure you. I have entertained guests – including a number of my fellow initiates – and sought no more than any man might wish: I sought peace.

But into this life my past associates have intruded. There is a small group of initiates who find themselves dissatisfied with the ambition of the Order. In this I might have been sympathetic but their hunger for power goes beyond the healthy acquisition of knowledge and the betterment of the self through Magick. They want to bring this whole country to its knees. They couldn't succeed of course, they have neither the intelligence or the drive, but they certainly do possess enough knowledge to cause a great deal of damage. Damage that you have no doubt already witnessed.

Of course a number of us have spoken out, have insisted that the Order police itself and drive these idiots into the gutter where they belong. But unfortunately they are well connected in the organisation, in fact they have the ear of Mathers himself, one of our founders and the closest the Order comes to a leader. In fact it was Mathers who issued the last threat to me. One which I have contemptuously ignored.

It was during a Christmas party I hosted recently for a few friends – I know, I know, a man such as I should have no time for such Christian celebrations, but at its roots it's pagan and I do so like gifts!

I hadn't invited Mathers, but when he arrived I saw no reason to turn him away. He had once been a friend to me and I felt I owed him a great deal during my couple of years in the Order.

"Samuel," I said, greeting him on the doorstep, "what a surprise."

He was charming and the perfect guest as we enjoyed an aperitif before dinner. The guests were a solid mixture, a couple of locals, poor Laura of course – she was always so devoted to me – Hilary De Montfort and a young friend of his... I forget the name, though he may have been Greek, or perhaps Turkish... There were enough for a party but not too many for dinner.

I had hired a piper of course, I am always a man for the full ceremony, and all was going delightfully.

We sat down for dinner, Wilkinson had prepared a splendid menu and I had hopes that the evening may provide a reconciliation. But then we came to the dessert course.

It was as inoffensive as a sweet can be, a rhubarb syllabub, but as the diners began to eat, panic erupted around the table. The cream was bubbling as if it were hot mud; one gentleman, having already consumed a mouthful began to cry out in panic as it worked its magic on his insides. I believe he is now on the road to recovery, though that night he vomited so much blood we assumed he wouldn't last until the next bells.

The sickly mess overflowed in its bowls and seeped into the tablecloth, burning the fabric and eating into the wood of the table itself. In the end the only way we could rid ourselves of the vile stuff was to carry the table out into the courtyard and burn it.

Throughout, Mathers had chuckled at his little game – for certainly it was down to him – only drawing me to one side as we stood on the lawn, listening to that hellish soup fizz and burn in the fire.

"A little humour," he said, his voice as thin and crackling as the embers of the wooden table that smouldered in front of us, "but also a point to be made. You are a target, young man, you have made yourself one as surely as if you had painted a bullseye on your chest. There is nowhere you can hide, not here, not halfway around the world. Wherever you are we will come calling and we will end your interference."

He held his hands out towards the fire to warm them. There was not enough fire in the world that could warm Samuel Mathers.

"It's Christmas," he said, "enjoy yourself, relax. But on the twenty-seventh we come calling. You may think you can fight us, and perhaps you can, for a while, but be sure: we will kill you in the end. We will kill you so hard your soul never stops screaming."

And with that he walked down the lawn towards the Loch, just strolled away as if out on an evening constitutional. I haven't seen him since. But I have certainly felt him.

He was true to his word and the next few days passed without incident. The snow fell and I took to my skis, resolving that if I were to die before the year was out, I would at the least enjoy the little time I had left.

Then came the evening of the twenty-seventh and I confess my nerves were not at their best.

I had prepared as best I could, enacting a number of protective spells and visualisations. I had spent the morning walking the periphery of the estate, all thirty-six acres of it, and placing protective charms along the boundary. I had also, not blind to the efficacy of brute force as well as spiritual defences, planted a number of steel traps and tripwires. I doubted the attack, when it came, would be so direct as to be a group of Mathers' acolytes marching through my gardens, but I was also only too aware that a Magickal attack is stronger when its practitioners are close by. I wished to prepare for anything.

At midnight, with still no overt sign of attack, I retired to my bedroom, reasoning that I could defend myself there as well as anywhere.

Eventually, sat up in an easy chair, the better part of a decanter of brandy inside me, I dozed off. For how long I cannot say, but when I awoke it was to the certainty that there was something outside my room that wished to gain entrance. There was a snuffling at the wood, such as a pig might make in its trough, nosing its way through its feed. Heavy claws, not the sharp weapons of a cat but rather the uneven, thick nails of a badger, scratched at the floorboards. They made a sound like a carpenter planing wood, the soft peel of layers, the squeal of splitting knots.

I began the Invocation of Attilus, a protection spell relied upon by many throughout the centuries. It is said that the spell places the man who casts it just a few moments ahead in time, where nobody can lay a finger on him as he is always just out of reach.

Certainly the atmosphere of the room became disturbed. The heavy grandfather clock that stands in the corridor outside my bedroom seemed to lose its rhythm, or perhaps it was me that was losing time with it, as the small area around me shifted its location in reality. The chair behind me began to warp, as if a pane of glass had been placed halfway through it to distort the view of its other half. The rug beneath my bare feet began to move, the strands of wool writhing like blades of grass in high wind.

Outside the door the creature roared. It was a roar that belied the size of it, it must have done, for it was so loud, so deep and terrifying that it couldn't have come from a creature small enough to fit in the corridor. It was a roar that sounded as big as the thunder we get here in the mountains, the deep reverberation of gods as they move across the skies. It was a roar that made the door creak in its frame like the deck of a ship in a storm. I felt sure that nothing I could do would be powerful enough to defend me from such a beast.

And yet, even as the door fell inwards and a wave of darkness forced its way into my room, the barrier around me held strong. No matter how big this creature was, no matter how powerful, I wasn't quite in the fold of reality that it prowled. I was just those few vital seconds ahead.

It reached out, a thick arm of pure shadow that bent and flexed against the distorting air around me. It hit the barrier as if it were made of solid glass, dissipating against its surface and widening like spilled wine soaking into the clean white linen of a tablecloth. It swirled all around me but could not gain access. I was safe. And I stayed that way until just before dawn when the darkness retreated from the cold white light of the thin, winter sun as it bounced off the snow outside my window.

I had survived the first night.

I went outside to survey the grounds and check the traps. All seemed undisturbed until, on the banks of the Loch, I came across the body

of Old Jamie, a local character known for his poaching habits and capacity for rough liquor. He would drink no more, he had been ground into the earth as if run over by a freight train, parts of his body mashed so thin it was impossible not to think of his skin as a worn bag that kept the rest of him together.

The creature – for I can only imagine that is what it was – had taken a victim so as not to return to Hell empty handed. I should have felt remorse but I will be honest with you gentlemen, I was only too glad it hadn't been me.

As I am sure you are aware, Magick is a complex art and a very movable one. The fear that lay ahead for me was that the spell that had saved my life was no longer of any use. Magickal combat is a game of development and a spell will only work once. When night fell I would, no doubt, face death again, but this time I would have to think of another way to avoid it.

The day brought more snow and the grounds gleamed so brightly with it, it was as if the gardens were glowing. I walked the boundary as I had the day before, more to clear my head than for any practical purpose. I was repeating a mantra I have often found useful for completely compartmentalising my thoughts. It is undeniable that the key to Magick is focus and that most failures to perform a spell or invocation are as a direct result of a cluttered mind.

I returned to the house to find the news that poor Hilary De Montfort had been killed during the night. There was no doubt in my mind on reading the initial reports that it was the work of Mathers and his followers. It was also alarming proof of the forces he had called upon to aid him in his desire for control and power. There is a huge division in the potency and pliability of the spirits and presences a man can conjure, but to vent something like the Breath of God, a force of divine retribution... To bring something so terrible into the world merely to use it as a weapon. The arrogance of that was something that astonished me... For Mathers to think this was something he could control...

Of course the other question was why he hadn't used that power against me rather than the dark spirit he had cast. Wishing no ill will towards Hilary, killing him with so potent a conjuration was rather like swatting a fly with a plank of wood. Hilary's skills were minor, he had little with which he could defend himself. In truth, were it not for his social position and his disarming enthusiasm, he wouldn't even have been a member of the Order. Why then had Mathers killed him in the way he had? To send a message? To scare those who stood against him? But why not use that power against me? It was some hours before the answer occurred to me.

The conjuration of a force such as the Breath of God is something that cannot easily be achieved. It would take the focus and energy of several practitioners working in close harmony. I had no doubt that such an invocation would have taken its toll on Mathers, even when the force had been used for such a brief and relatively easy task as killing Hilary or the unfortunate Lord Ruthvney. If he had sent the force against me, not only would he have had to focus his energy across great distances, he would also have had a fight on his hands. I am not arrogant enough to suggest it is a fight he would not have won. I may be a great adept, but the Breath of God is something that I could not imagine facing alone. Still, it would have placed a great strain on him, something he would not have wanted in the earliest stages of his plans. Indeed, perhaps it would bode well for the attack to come? I felt sure I wouldn't be facing him at his strongest.

Despite this hope I had no wish to expire through complacency and I spent the rest of the day in my temple, preparing myself both mentally and physically for the night ahead. I decided to make use of the piece of Bartholomew's Chalk I had bought in India. It is said to be constructed with holy water as well as the powdered bones of a creature only found in one of the outer dimensions. Each piece costs a king's ransom but what price can one put on survival?

Whether or not the ingredients were quite as advertised, the chalk was unquestionably potent. I had to use fire tongs to hold it and the lines it drew burned themselves into the wooden floorboards. Within the valleys of the shape I placed bowls filled with a solution composed of my own blood combined with that of a stillborn lamb, the innocence of the latter intended to cancel out the nefariousness of the former!

As the sky began to darken I stepped within the pentacle and began to recite the Glayven Principle, an incantation designed to purify the air immediately around the speaker.

It was some hours before I began to suspect something was amiss. The words of the Glayven Principle had been echoing back at me all the while. The acoustics in the room I have made my temple are particularly pleasing, and there is a lovely hypnotic reverberation that I find most beneficial when wishing to enter a trance state. It became clear, however, that the echo was stretching, becoming more and more delayed. At first I suspected that the attack was – as a counterpoint to my defence of the night before – on time itself. Perhaps Mathers wished to preternaturally age me, or even the reverse? I had heard of such rituals being used before but never seen them successfully practiced.

However, the attack was a lot simpler in nature. From the shadows that lingered at all sides of me, the echo began to clarify as a separate voice. I could hear footsteps, the slow and deliberate tread of a man with all the time in the world, circling me just beyond the reach of the candlelight.

"I hear you," I called into the shadows. "Show yourself!"

"I am not someone you wish to look on," came the voice, and it was the mirror of my own, just as the echo had been. "To look on me would invite madness."

"It will take more than your voice to snap my mind," I replied. "I am more resilient than you give me credit for."

"Very well," it replied and stepped into the light. The face, like the voice, was my own.

"Handsome fellow," I joked – for sometimes it's important to show bravery in the face of demons. "I can assure you that is a face I have no problem looking on."

"We shall see," it replied, stripping naked and sitting down opposite me, as close as the pentacle would allow.

"Now," it said picking up a small blade from the pocket of its discarded jacket, "let us see how long I can make this last."

And slowly it began to unmake itself, picking and peeling at the mirror-image of my body as I looked on. And I couldn't help but look, as much as I tried to avert my gaze I found that I was paralysed, unable to do more than blink as the grotesque show played out for me. It was a business that took it hours, removing each piece of skin, carving each muscle, paring the flesh down unto the very bone itself. It left the head until last so that I was never able to forget whose body was being so corrupted. I watched my face scream itself hoarse until, eventually, it cut out the tongue and all that was left was the noise of animal retching as it whittled away at the little that was left.

By that time I felt closer to madness than ever before.

What was left of me – and I could no longer think of it as anything other than myself – a chattering collection of bones, placed the knife with its blade almost touching the wall of my pentacle. The inference was obvious: now it was my turn.

And despite every ounce of self-preservation in me, my hand slowly began to reach for the knife. I couldn't control myself, it was as if a law of nature demanded I complete the butchery demanded. Fight as I did, my fingers kept moving towards the edge of the pentacle and the knife. I did the only thing I could think of, I began to choke myself, starving the brain of oxygen in the hope that I could pass out and, therefore, move beyond the spirit's influence. My vision swam as I hyperventilated and then exhaled with my one loyal hand clamped over my mouth and nose. My head burst with pain and I toppled back to the floor, hitting my head with a sound blow as I did so, which no doubt helped my endeavour.

When I came back to consciousness the light was beginning to show through the window behind me and I managed not to look as the mirror image of my bones somehow managed to pull themselves together and walk out of the room. They made a sound like dominoes rattled in their sack.

My head ached, abominably, so I lay there a little while longer.

After Crowley finished speaking there were a few moments of silence while his tale was absorbed. Then he spoke once more, chilling words that caused the temperature in the room to drop even further:

"So," he said, "all that remains is to wonder what excitement awaits us tonight!"

CHAPTER EIGHTEEN

A LETTER

EXCERPT FROM A LETTER WRITTEN BY DR JOHN WATSON TO
SHERLOCK HOLMES

Well, you did warn me that matters were likely to get stranger! I have told you as much of Crowley's story as I can recall, I would have made notes but it seemed rude in the circumstances and so I had to rely on my memory. The story was certainly unusual and startling enough for me to state with some certainty that it is accurate, though I admit I may have got the odd detail (such as the names of the rituals) wrong. It seems to me to confirm something of what we know, however, namely the ring I found in the forest by Ruthvney Hall. "To S.L.M.M." it said, might I suggest that to be "Samuel Liddell MacGregor Mathers"? At least one piece of this puzzle falls securely into place.

You asked that I should be prepared to believe, I have since begun to wonder why. If you had been sat in Crowley's drawing room during the telling of his tale you would hardly have been able to remain silent. I am sure you would have been deeply sceptical of all he said. It occurs to me that that is why you made yourself absent: some of us can remain politely silent in the face of things we disbelieve, others must make themselves heard!

I will confess that while a great deal of what Crowley said sounded entirely implausible, I am no longer of a mind to dismiss it as readily as before. The experience on the train still hangs over me and try as I might to find a logical explanation I cannot. And if that was exactly what it seemed then did Crowley's experiences sound any stranger?

I give up trying to form an opinion, I will deal with matters as they come. I pass on the information and you must make of it what you will.

If Crowley's long speech was full of arcane terminology and references, it was nothing compared to the response from Carnacki.

"You said you bought this house in order to perform a ritual," he said, "might I ask which one?"

"Certainly, it is the Abramelin Ritual, Boleskine fits all the necessary geographical prerequisites."

"The Abramelin Ritual?" Carnacki asked, seemingly incensed by the idea. "Are you mad?"

"I take it this ritual is dangerous?" I asked.

"The Abramelin Ritual is a process whereby the darkest powers imaginable are contacted and brought into our world."

"And forced to do good," Crowley countered. "That is rather the point is it not?"

"'Forced?'" shouted Carnacki. "'Did you not recently accuse Mathers of such blind arrogance? The thought that you could control something so primal, so ludicrously dangerous? You, sir, are a bloody idiot!"

"And you are a guest in my house," Crowley replied, calmly, yet with a force that made it quite clear he was not a man one would would wish to have as an enemy. "So please have a care."

Carnacki, unwilling to back down, did at least have the good sense to change his tone. "It is not just I that need have a care," he said, softly, "should the ritual not go as planned then we will all be in dire peril."

"The ritual will not fail."

Carnacki, only too aware that he would be wasting his time arguing further, concluded the conversation.

"All of this is beside the point," Dr Silence declared, "for if we are not able to assist in your surviving the night, you will hardly be in a position to complete the ritual."

"True enough," Crowley agreed, "but it's not just a case of tonight, we need to take the fight to Mathers and his people before they unleash Hell on us all." He looked to me. "If only your colleague was still with us, Dr Watson, I fear that while he concentrates on the minutiae of this case, he is blind to the greater concerns: if Mathers and his allies aren't stopped, it won't be the death of a couple of nobles that concern us, it'll be the death of whole nations."

"And what do you suggest we do, sir?" I asked. "We can hardly go to the police, not with a story like yours."

"Precisely why Holmes would have been an asset," Silence said, "with his connections both in the police force and, indeed, the government itself, we might just have been in a position to act."

"Well," said Carnacki, "he isn't here so might I suggest we concentrate on the assets we do have? There are only a few hours until sunset and from thereafter we will likely have a fight on our hands. If Mathers is worth his salt at all he must have spies reporting for him –

Hell, a simple scrying ritual would tell him – he must know that you are no longer alone in this fight."

I didn't dare ask what a scrying ritual might be, only too aware that I would neither like nor understand the answer.

"Indeed," Crowley agreed, "it is most fortunate that we have such a skilled army on our side. I dared not share my concerns with any other members of the Order, who could tell where their allegiance might lie? But clearly we have no need of them, your abilities combined with ours should give Mathers pause. We shall soon number one more, then our ranks will be complete. I contacted another associate of mine, an expert in demonology. In fact," he glanced at his watch, "he should be with us within the hour. Until then may I suggest we prepare our borders!"

It cannot fail to surprise you that there was little for me to do. It was a distinctly odd sensation as an ex-soldier, watching these three men dashing around preparing a major defensive operation but not with guns, barricades or explosives but rather mounds of salt, chalk marks on the wainscoting and a liberal spraying of what I took to be holy water. It was quite ridiculous. And yet terrifying also, because the earnestness with which they went about the task allowed me no room for doubt: they were preparing to fight for their – *our* – lives.

Crowley's final guest arrived. He was a small, portly figure with hair that made up for what it lacked on top by flapping about at the sides of his egg-shaped head. The only concession to his... (what? Hobby? Vocation? How is one to describe these people?) was a Mephistophelean beard, black and coming to a point at the chin that lifted towards his nose. It was quite the most bizarre facial hair I have ever seen.

"Ah!" announced Crowley, greeting the man with an overjoyed

embrace. "So we are all together! My friends meet the foremost expert in demonology and ancient curses in the country, if not the world: Mr Julian Karswell."

Karswell gave a little bow. "I must say, Aleister," he said in a voice that was every bit as feline as his poise, for despite his shape he moved with considerable grace, "this was all terribly inconvenient. I was due to host my annual party for the local children today, they do so love my conjuring tricks. And my mother's ice cream of course..." He looked at all of us in turn. "Such a gathering," he said. "Dr Silence I know, of course, and, correct me if I'm wrong, but you seem familiar..." He looked to me. "Is it not the writer? Watley, Whates..."

"Watson," I said, not wanting to watch him struggle indefinitely, "and I'm a doctor really, writing's just a hobby."

"Really? Oh but you must know a few people in the business I dare say, I would so love to discuss it with you. I have a book that I've just completed you see, *A History of Witchcraft*, the definitive word on the subject, rather."

"Sounds fascinating," I said, lying through my teeth of course, "but I really only know magazine publishers I'm afraid, and I'm not sure it's the sort of thing that they..."

"Oh indeed not," agreed Karswell, "never mind. I had just thought a review or two... One doesn't like to send it to too many places, especially not to those who would not be receptive... I'm really not a man who warms to criticism... And you are?" He looked to Carnacki.

"Thomas Carnacki, another expert in demonology, still I dare say you can't have too many."

"An expert, eh? One would have said you were too young. Yes, far too young."

"I might surprise you."

"Indeed you might. Very well," Karswell looked to Crowley, "shall we begin then?"

And thus, the preparations continued, with the new arrival chipping in his views on the matter. I decided it was by far the best idea for me to stay out of the way. I had McGillicuddy order up some sandwiches and I've polished those off while writing this to you. Soon it will be dark, the night falls quick and early this far north I imagine. Then... Well, then, we shall just have to see won't we?

More later. One hopes.

CHAPTER NINETEEN

THE BATTLE OF BOLESKINE

Having long since missed the opportunity to get a letter into Foyers to meet the post, I finished the section I had written, folded the paper neatly and hid it in my bag.

I sipped the last of a pot of coffee that had come with the sandwiches and then descended to the "temple" to see how matters had progressed.

I felt very much surplus to requirements, a man with none of the skills that were needed for the business ahead. I knew that Carnacki viewed me as a liability, a weak link that should be locked up in one of the rooms where I couldn't get in the way or provide an easy target for whatever might come. I sympathised with his stance, hearkening back to my military days when the last thing I would have wanted in the middle of a tense mission was a civilian getting under our feet. Still, I was determined that, as someone who was as yet uncertain as to his beliefs in the occult and the threat represented by Samuel Mathers and his confederates, I should witness all and be the conclusive voice of reason.

I found the four men in varying degrees of readiness, a large star shape – the aforementioned pentacle, I presumed – was drawn on the floor and there lingered the distinct smell of burning wood and wax. I could only imagine that the floorboards had been singed once again. Each man was working to his own method:

Dr Silence, his lips chattering away silently within the confines of his beard, appeared to be approaching matters purely internally. He stood facing one of the star's five points reciting whatever incantation gave him strength, occasionally tapping his finger against the seam of his trousers as if counting stanzas.

Crowley was every inch the theatre satanist, dressed in flowing purple robes. He chanted loudly in Latin, dropping small nuggets of incense into a glowing censer. The incense flared and gave off balls of sweet-smelling white smoke. Looking at his eyes I could tell from his pupils that he had taken some form of drug. I recognised the look well enough from Holmes' dark days. I would later read an article by Crowley insisting that heavy drug use was an important part of achieving the correct mental state with which to conduct rituals. An article that did his credulity no favours at all in the eyes of the medical fraternity.

Karswell appeared to be scribbling a series of foreign letters onto thick strips of parchment. Each piece would be carefully allowed to dry before being stacked in a small pile near the centre of the pentacle.

Finally, Carnacki, who approached the business of demons like a scientist. He had wired a set of linked glass tubes to a large wooden box. And was currently loading a heavy revolver with cartridges containing rock salt and silver, a powerful calibre against the forces of darkness, he insisted.

"Gentlemen," I said, not wishing to interrupt those mid-prayer but feeling I should announce myself.

"Stand inside the pentacle," Carnacki said, "and keep quiet."

"Very well." I did as I was told, well, almost. "Might I also have some cartridges?" I asked holding up my service revolver. "I think you'll find they fit my Enfield."

"But can you shoot?"

"I am likely a far better shot than you," I said with a smile.

For once from Carnacki the smile was returned and he handed me a box of the custom-made bullets. "Maybe you'll earn your place after all."

We took our positions in silence, each staring out from one of the five points of the pentangle. It could hardly have been planned better, I thought to myself. If Holmes had been here we would have been one too many.

Slowly the natural light began to dim, the candles growing ever more potent as the shadows around them deepened.

I had noticed earlier the large terrace off Crowley's temple, accessed from a north-facing set of French windows. The terrace had been coated in a thick layer of sand dredged from the banks of the Loch. When I had asked him why, he explained it was so that he could discern the footsteps of the demons that came to visit, even though they might be invisible to the human eye. I wondered now if ancient feet were leaving their indentations, if forces were creeping closer.

Within ten minutes or so the darkness was complete.

Crowley had insisted that the servants retire to their quarters and not leave them. Working for such a man I was sure they were used to this command. Which meant that when we heard sounds from the long corridor outside, we couldn't mistake them for anything other than a sign of intruders.

"Steady now," said Silence, holding out his hands and taking long, slow breaths, "the first wave is here."

The noises were faint to begin with, the jangle of metal against metal, the tap of something hard on the floorboards. Then, after a few moments, the sounds coalesced and the raging drum of horses hooves came clattering along the corridor.

"The Angel of Death?" asked Crowley.

"Or just a horse spirit," replied Carnacki. "Let's wait until we clap eyes on it, shall we?"

"If it's the Angel of Death, that's the last thing you want to do," said Karswell.

"Ah," said Carnacki waving the comment away dismissively, "it won't be the first time I've looked that bony old revenant in the eye sockets."

The sound of hooves rose to such a terrifying volume that I had to squint against the persistent hammering. Books and ornaments fell from the tables and shelves as the house shook.

Then it appeared! A translucent figure, recognisably a horse but with something on its back: wet, chain-mailed feet pressed into chinking stirrups, a bare torso, more ribs than flesh, a skull of a face, its tombstone teeth chattering like a telegraph key hammering out a message.

"Allow me," said Silence, who had continued to mutter under his breath throughout the last exchange. He raised his hands further and, though his body blocked a clear view, I swear it seemed as if two blazing figures burst from his chest. Both built seemingly from flames, the first was in the shape of a dog, a mid-sized animal, a Border Collie perhaps. The other was clearly a cat, its tail crooked into a question mark and its mouth opened wide to issue a sulphurous hiss.

"Dear God!" shouted Karswell. "Are they spirit guardians?"

Silence didn't reply immediately, it was clear that he was concentrating on maintaining the animal creatures he had conjured forth. "Smoke and Flame," he said eventually, his voice strained, "my animal spirits, the embodiment of two of my most loyal and courageous friends." He gave a roar, throwing forward his arms, the fingers splayed awkwardly, twisted almost as if broken. "Fight it!" he shouted, and the creatures did so.

The dog chased around behind the creature on horseback, rearing up to tear at its shimmering flanks with its front claws. The cat leapt straight for the rider, pushing its sleek nose into its chest cavity and climbing upwards, a raging orange light shining out from the skull's eyes, nose and mouth like the glow of a jack-o'-lantern.

The horse rose up onto its back legs, but Flame, the dog spirit, jumped higher, its fiery teeth snapping at the creature's exposed belly. There was a shower of gelatinous matter that brought to mind the ectoplasm web in the dining carriage and then Smoke, the cat spirit, burst from the skeletal neck, the rider's head shattering as the ball of fire exploded it from within.

There was a patter as the cooling embers rained down onto the floorboards, then all was silent but for the flickering sound of Flame and Smoke. Both creatures were sat on the floor now, their heat somehow not scorching the wood.

"Thank you, my friends," said Silence and, as a pair, they jumped towards him and vanished.

"Round one?" I asked.

"Well and truly won," Carnacki said then, looking down at my shoes he waved a cautionary hand. "Keep your feet well inside the line," he said, "a fraction of you crosses that barrier and you're no longer protected. Worse still, you rub a gap in the chalk and we're all wide open to attack."

"Right," I said, suitably admonished. "Sorry, you must remember I am new to this."

"Pray you live long enough to get used to it," Silence said.

His eyes had taken on a dreamy quality and it was obvious from his stance that the effort of defending us against the first attack had taken a lot out of him. "I think I'll let someone else take charge of the next one," he said. "It will be all I can manage to stay upright for a while."

"Let's hope we have a little time to recover," said Karswell, "I would rather we were all in a fit state to..."

He stopped speaking as a faint noise began to grow louder. It was a strange, high-pitched screech, the closest analogy I can think of is the noise a gramophone needle makes when slipping in the groove of a record. The room grew even darker as the noise grew louder, eventually we could no longer see the opposite walls and were stranded within an island of light cast by the closest candles.

In the darkness, at a point that seemed much too far away from us to still be in the room, a pinprick of light appeared and I began to wonder if that noise were not the sound made when something tries to force its way into our world.

"No rest for the blessed," Carnacki said. "What is that?"

"Oh no..." Karswell whispered. "It can't be..."

"What, man?" Crowley snapped. "We haven't time for indecision. If you know what it is then act!"

The pinprick of light was slowly widening, unfolding even, into a tiny plume of smoke. That smoke began to grow as if, just on the other side of that sheet of space, there was an infernal engine getting its steam up.

"But there must be something attracting it!" said Karswell. "It requires a focus, a beacon to draw its power!"

"There's nothing in the pentacle but ourselves," said Carnacki, "and why would any of us draw this thing here?"

The smoke continued to unfold, becoming a larger and larger ball that hovered in the distance.

"Empty your pockets!" insisted Karswell. "All of you!"

We did as he asked, casting things onto the floor in the centre of the pentangle. Loose change, a couple of pocket knives, pipes, tobacco... all the usual gentlemanly belongings.

"Wait," I said. "What's this?" I held up a small piece of black card that I had found in the inside pocket of my jacket. "I swear I have never seen it before," I said, "it must have been slipped in there while I was unaware."

"Easy enough done," said Karswell, "but the point is: can I get rid of it?"

For a bizarre moment the piece of paper lifted into the air entirely of its own volition and it seemed that Karswell would have no need to dispose of it for it would vanish itself.

"No you don't," said Carnacki, snatching it from the air as if it were a troublesome mosquito. "How do you negate the effect of it?" he Karswell asked.

"You don't!" the smaller man insisted. "All you can do is pass it back to the person that gave it to you in the first place. Once the rune is cast, it cannot be revoked. The demon will hunt it forever!"

"Then I should run," I said, mindful of how large the ball of smoke was getting, "draw it away from the rest of you."

"Noble as ever, Doctor," said Carnacki with a smile, "but Karswell will think of something. Won't you?"

The air of delicate gentility that Karswell had previously shown appeared to be crumbling with the panic. He looked to Crowley, then back to us, then to the smoke that was now almost twice the size of a man. Lights flickered at the heart of it, like the spitting tip of a metal sparkler.

"Yes," Karswell said finally, following my eyes towards where the demon was manifesting. "Give me the paper."

Carefully making sure it didn't fly away again, Carnacki did just that. Karswell held the fragment by the tip and I marvelled to see it worm around as if alive.

"Get me some of his blood," Karswell said.

"Some of my —" I began, but Crowley had already gripped my hand and, pulling a curved knife from somewhere within his purple robes, he drew the blade across my palm, opening a thin cut in the skin. Karswell took my bleeding hand by the wrist and dipped the tip of the wriggling paper into the blood. It soaked it up like litmus paper, the dull surface turning shiny gloss as it dampened.

"Right," Karswell said, keeping his eye on the smoke.

"Quickly, man!" Carnacki shouted, pointing to the floor where a large black footprint, almost like that of a three-toed lizard, burned itself into the wood.

"*Eetz inti treiz*," mumbled Karswell, in a language I didn't recognise.

"It's coming!" shouted Silence.

"And it's not the only thing!" cried Carnacki as a grotesque, swinish noise became audible over that stylus screech. "John!" It took me a moment to realise he meant me. "Get ready to fire!"

Another three-toed footprint burned into the wooden floor.

"*Veesh lamma hyze!*" Karswell continued in that strange dialect.

There was something appearing in the smoke, something covered in thick, dark hair, its horns straight like an alpine goat's. It was running towards us, getting bigger and bigger as it sprinted along the impossible tunnel that was opening between Crowley's house and whatever awful realm it came from.

"*Ryad, kamma lan tash!*" Karswell roared, the blood-soaked piece of paper vanishing from between his fingers.

The running creature faded as, slowly, the smoke began to shrink once more, folding back in on itself until it was nothing but the size of a golfball, those brilliant, shining sparks glistening at its centre. Then nothing. The tunnel was gone.

"The paper was you," said Karswell, out of breath, drained just as Silence had been. "Transportation spell, somewhere far away..."

"You mean that thing's just going to burst out of nowhere in the midst of some poor innocents?" I asked, terrified that our problem had now become someone else's.

"Problems of our own!" shouted Crowley as the snuffling noises grew louder and, out of the darkness that surrounded us, several small, grey figures appeared. They were troll-like in appearance, snouted, with long, yellow teeth that sat uncomfortably in their mouths. They moved slowly, their great weight surely making it hard for them to manoeuvre.

Carnacki fired, the bullet hitting the foremost and making a hole that melted around the edges, a grotesque, purple cream gushing from its centre. The creature fell and oozed away. Carnacki took another shot, and another...

"We need to take this in turns," he said to me. "I fire, then you, with each of us reloading while the other keeps them back." He fired again. "Are you ready?"

"As I'll ever be," I said, standing next to him and weighing the Enfield in my hand.

"Good." Carnacki smiled, and took his last two shots. "Go!"

I stepped forward, aimed, and slowly, calmly, took my six shots, timing it to coincide with the time it took Carnacki to load. With the last, I dropped to one knee and lined the shot to hit two of the creatures. I had no idea if the bullet would pass through both but felt it worth a try. It did, they may have been big but they were also soft.

"Show-off," said Carnacki, but I could tell he was beginning to thaw towards me, not that I particularly craved his endorsement, I'd be happy just to survive the night. I had already shaken a handful of cartridges from the box in my jacket pocket into my hand and I ejected the spent casings and reloaded before Carnacki had taken his fifth shot.

I am particularly good at two things in life: being a soldier and being a doctor, taking lives and saving them. The irony doesn't amuse me one bit.

"He must tire soon," said Crowley, "this is leagues beyond his previous efforts."

"He knows there are many of us," responded Carnacki, reloading while I took my turn, "and this..." he gestured towards the creatures, "this is just cannon fodder, keeping us distracted before the next big threat."

As if on cue, the ground shook. Karswell fell to the floor, cursing as some of his little pieces of paper fluttered around him.

"What was that?" asked Silence.

"At a guess," I replied, taking my six shots quickly, "the next big threat."

The ground shook again and we could hear the sound of breaking glass from somewhere along the corridor.

The creatures were coming in greater numbers now, more than Carnacki and I could manage with just the two guns.

Picking himself up, Karswell stepped alongside us, muttering under his breath, folding his little pieces of paper and pitching them towards the creatures. The paper pellets hit like small grenades, blowing holes in the creatures as surely as our bullets. Silence came to the fore also, not manifesting his animal spirits this time but instead sending percussive blasts of air from the tips of his fingers that had the same effect as both bullets and pellets.

Once more, the room shook as something large, something terrible, came our way.

"I need you to cover for me," said Carnacki, as he reached for the glass tubes he had been connecting earlier. He looked to Crowley as he screwed them together. "You're not being much help," he said, "this is your battle, remember?"

I didn't hear Crowley's reply, I was too busy taking my turn at shooting the creatures that continued to flood towards us.

Boom. The earth shook again. This time the candelabra actually left the ground, all jumping half a foot or so before dropping back with a resounding thud. The candles flickered, a couple extinguishing, dropping us into even greater darkness.

"Nearly ready," said Carnacki behind me, "nearly ready."

The tide of small creatures ceased, the last falling to one of Silence's flicks of compressed air. "Wait for a target," he said, hands extended, long fingers twitching.

Karswell took the opportunity to create more ammunition, scribbling sets of runes on more blank parchment. He set great stock by the effects of these "words of power", and having seen them in action, I couldn't help but agree.

Another tremor, and the dawning certainty that there was *something* out there in the dark. A warm gust of air passed over us, a breath I realised, that brought with it the sweet, straw stench of an animal cage in a zoo.

"It's right here!" shouted Karswell.

"Not for long," insisted Carnacki, flicking a switch on the large wooden box that sat by his feet. There was a brief whine that built into a solid, low hum. In his hands the glass tubes were now constructed as a mirror of the chalk shape we stood in. Surrounded by a fan of metal shutters, the tubes glowed brightly, powered by the acid battery in the wooden box, cables hanging between the two as he strode forward. "The Electric Pentacle," he explained, his face bathed in the blue light the device cast. "A weapon of my own design, the gas in the tubes has mystical properties, the light it casts is hugely powerful." He moved to the furthest point in the pentangle. "It burns," he said finally, pointing the pentangle out towards the darkness and flipping a large brass switch that dangled from one of the wires hanging around him.

The light from the Electric Pentacle pulsed and Carnacki triggered a switch at the rear of the device that brought the shutters down, surrounding the tubes like the petals of a flower, focusing their light in a steady beam directly into the darkness.

For a brief second we all caught a glimpse of the creature that was out there as the light reflected off its many black eyes, and the quivering mass of ganglia it sported where its mouth should be. Then there was nothing but the blue light, and the ground shook once more as the creature returned to wherever it had come from.

Carnacki gave a short cry as the Electric Pentacle began to smoke in his hands. "The cables!" he shouted, getting tangled in them. "Disconnect!"

I yanked the two, heavy-duty wires from the top of the wooden box and the light immediately cut out.

Carnacki slowly lowered the whole device to the floor and stepped back, waving his burned hands in the air. "Needs a bit more work," he admitted.

"Seems just fine to me," I said, "it's certainly effective."

Carnacki nodded. "True, but if it had exploded, I'm not completely sure it wouldn't have torn a hole in the fabric of reality and that wouldn't have been good."

"What's wrong with Crowley?" asked Silence suddenly, dashing over to where the man had fallen flat on his back.

"He is possessed," said Karswell, stepping back slightly as Crowley's body began to shake. "What did you do to him?" he asked Carnacki.

"Me?" Carnacki was clearly affronted. "What makes you think I did anything?"

"You were the last to talk to him."

"I merely asked him why he wasn't taking a very active role – a fair comment!"

"Gentlemen," I said, grabbing Crowley's arm and feeling for a pulse, "now is hardly the time."

Crowley appeared to be experiencing some form of seizure, his teeth clenched, his brow furrowed. Beads of sweat trickled down his face as he thrashed around on the floor.

"Dear Lord!" I moved back slightly, startled by the sight of his body beginning to swell beneath the purple robes.

"What is happening to him?" Karswell shouted. "He's inflating like a damned balloon!"

Silence moved forward, pushing between Crowley and I. "Forgive me, Doctor," he said, "but this may be a matter that requires more than medical knowledge."

Feeling it was hardly constructive to fight the man over it, I stepped back and allowed him room.

He held Crowley down as the robes continued to swell, as if he were filling up from the inside.

"The Breath of God!" declared Karswell. "It must be!"

Crowley's eyes flickered open and he roared at the ceiling. The experience was incredible, a wind that raged through the room, knocking over the candelabra, smashing the censers and extinguishing the fires.

"It's here!" Crowley shouted. "Help me push it —"

There was a sudden silence. The darkness was empty for a few moments then a match was struck illuminating Carnacki's face. I heard him elevating one of the toppled candelabra and then watched as he relit the candles.

"Gone," whispered Crowley. "It's gone."

"You destroyed it?" I asked.

Crowley shook his head. "Just sent it elsewhere, released it..."

"Released it?" Carnacki was beside himself with rage. "You've let it loose?"

Crowley nodded and Carnacki looked as deflated as I had ever seen him. "Then who knows how many will die before we might contain it once more."

CHAPTER TWENTY

A Letter (Continued)

Excerpt From a Letter Written by Dr John Watson to Sherlock Holmes

I begin to think that this letter will never be posted.

Holmes, for all my favourable talk of the country it must be remembered that they have no infrastructure here. If I want to send you a message, I have to commit to half an hour's cart journey and a village post office that views opening times with the sort of loose informality that would have an urban business bankrupt within a week.

No matter, I can only hope that I will find the time when I arise later, for really, matters have come to a point and we need you here. I need you here. If only to tell me I'm dreaming.

I have explained to you, in as much detail as possible, the events of the night, our "battle" against whatever unbelievable forces they were that faced us across the dimensions. Oh dear Lord... I'm even beginning to talk like them. Holmes, you simply cannot imagine how terrifying it was. Worse, how quickly one stops questioning and just adapts. I was firing my service revolver at DEMONS, Holmes. My whole view of the world is in ruins.

And Mary. How can I not think of her? Now that I know that the veil between life and death is thinner than I imagined, now that I know that there are souls out there that are still *themselves*. I was somewhat ambivalent about the idea of an afterlife, Holmes, I think all soldiers are; have to be. But now I begin to wonder.

I miss her so very much.

Enough, forgive me, my friend, I know you find this sort of conversation awkward. Let's stick to the facts shall we?

Where had I got to…? Ah yes, Carnacki's concern that the Breath of God was now loose upon the world.

I cannot pretend I followed every aspect of their conversation. Once the battle was done – and it was, there were no more attacks after that – my adrenalin faded and I began to feel that same sense of disassociation I had experienced on the train. A dizziness and lethargy, nausea even. It was shock, I know, I am a medical man after all.

Still, despite my discomfort and confusion, I followed the generalities of their discussion. It seemed that Mathers' final act had been to send the Breath of God directly into Crowley. How he was able to do that I cannot say, the words of explanation simply slip off the brain. No doubt I adopted that vacant look Mary always had once I started to discuss anatomy. All you had to do to send that woman to sleep was speak Latin.

Explanations aside, that is what had happened. And in order to defend himself, Crowley had vented it elsewhere. Where, he could not say. He suspects London (in which case you will likely know more about it than me) because he tried to send it right back to its source. But he could not be certain.

As dawn broke it shone its light on five exhausted men. The only plan we had was to use a "scrying" ritual (don't ask) to try and locate the Breath of God, but apparently before that could even be considered all concerned needed to rest. Fighting psychically is – logically enough I suppose – extremely draining.

I confess that I was unsure as to whether I could possibly sleep after such an experience. In all honesty, though, as I write these words, I find I am struggling to stay awake. Perhaps it would be better were I to leave

CHAPTER TWENTY-ONE

HIS RETURN

I was shaken roughly awake by a hand on my shoulder.

"What?" I was extremely disorientated and despite the perfect brightness of the day that lit my room, it took me a few moments for my vision to clear. I rubbed at my face, aware that someone had awoken me, yet I could so easily have fallen back asleep, my mind was that sluggish.

"Have a drink of water," said a familiar voice, "it may help."

"Holmes?" I asked, my voice cracking, throat dry.

I looked over to find him sat beside me on the bed, propped up on my spare pillows. Scattered all over the bed and floor were pages of writing. My letter, I realised. I was about to remonstrate with him when he placed his finger to his lips and smiled.

"Keep your voice down, my friend," he said, "I have no wish to disturb the rest of the household as yet."

I took a drink of water as he had suggested, to clear my throat.

"You mean they don't know you're here?"

"I entered via your window," he gave a dry chuckle, "though I have left some of the most complex and absurd dance-patterns in the sand outside Crowley's temple, I'm afraid I just couldn't resist!"

"Oh Holmes..."

"Never mind that. I've read your letter and must say that I'm enthralled. What an adventure you've had."

"Perhaps you wouldn't have been so enthralled had you been forced to experience it. I have never been so..." Words failed me for a moment as a surge of emotion choked me. That was immediately replaced by a sense of extreme irritation. I knew my friend could hardly relate to such feelings and the last thing I wanted was to appear weak. I growled in anger and drank some more water, if only so as to engage myself with something that was neither speaking nor crying.

"I know," Holmes said gently, proving that he can at least have some empathy, "forgive me, I should not joke. But you must see that all of this represents the most intriguing set of circumstances to cross my path for years." He sparkled, as alive on the events he was mired in, glowing as bright as Carnacki's Electric Pentacle had the night before. He had the same violent excitement that he used to seek from cocaine, that fizzy stimulation that was his preferred state. It is a wonder to me Holmes was ever able to grow old, he really didn't have the hobbies for it.

"But do you believe it?" I asked, quietly, afraid of course of being made to feel foolish.

"I believe you saw every single thing you say you did," he replied, picking up a few stray pages of the letter and flinging them to the floor. "And I believe we are close to a resolution in all this."

"But the Breath of God..."

"Blows at the command of another," Holmes interrupted, "and that is where we must concentrate our energies."

He got to his feet. "I have observed from a distance for long enough. It's time I re-entered the fray," he announced, unlocking the window and swinging one wire-thin leg out of it. "But I shall do so via the front door, as a guest not a cat burglar."

And before I could say another word, he had dropped entirely from my sight.

It occurred to me to check my watch and I was startled to see it was already half past three in the afternoon. I had certainly been tired to have slept so long. In fact, if Holmes hadn't roused me, who knows how long I would have continued?

I rang McGillicuddy and asked for some hot water, also enquiring as to whether anyone else had arisen.

"No, sir," he said, his disdain almost completely hidden, "but that is not unusual in this household."

"I see," I replied, slightly awkwardly, "it must be difficult to run a household on such a chaotic timetable, eh?"

McGillicuddy eyed me with a sort of dilute incomprehension. "It is as the master wishes, sir," he said and left the room.

Once again I had failed to make friends with the staff.

I washed, dressed and went downstairs. Maybe I'd manage to find some breakfast. Or lunch. Or afternoon tea.

I had negotiated for a cold collation and was settling down in the dining room in anticipation of it when the front doorbell rang and, as expected, Holmes announced himself. I could only guess at McGillicuddy's professional confusion as he wondered how to announce a guest to a master who was resolutely asleep. He was saved the difficulty as I heard Crowley's voice echo across the entrance hall in greeting.

Soon they joined me in the dining room and I decided to be nice and affect surprise at seeing Holmes.

"How marvellous that you were able to make it," I said, "and so promptly! It seems no time at all since I last saw you."

Holmes smiled and took a seat at the head of the table. "I was forceful with Mycroft," he replied, "as you know I can usually wrap him around my finger when I need to."

That was hardly my experience of their relationship but I wasn't about to argue. Especially as Crowley's response was so enthusiastic.

"I am so pleased to hear it," he said, "because there is no doubt that we will have need of his assistance."

"Really?" Holmes replied, pretending to be completely in the dark. "What possible assistance can the government be in these matters?"

"Mr Holmes," said Crowley, "the entire country, nay the world itself, is in the most terrible danger and it is only through the actions of people like ourselves that it can be safeguarded."

He proceeded to tell Holmes everything that had happened, with particular emphasis on the fact that Samuel Mathers and his colleagues within the Golden Dawn were poised to attack and time was of the essence.

"Then let us act," said Holmes. "You say yourself that this is a business in which experts are needed, you are those experts, so do what needs to be done."

"But without the support and approval of the government? These are important people we are rallied against. I hardly exaggerate when I say that some of them have the ear of the Queen herself."

He began to reel off a list of names and I can confirm that he did not exaggerate. According to Crowley, the perpetrators of this scheme were amongst the very best of society. He listed businessmen, statesmen, figures of such unassailable pedigree I began to fear even more how we were ever to succeed against them.

"And you have proof?" asked Holmes.

"Mr Holmes, we experienced the proof last night, it is only thanks to the extreme efforts of all concerned that we survived to fight another day."

"With all due respect," said Holmes, "being attacked in such a manner hardly proves the identity of your attackers. Is there nothing to show a conclusive link between these names and the actions you ascribe to them?"

"If there was then I would hardly be appealing to you! Mathers wishes to stage nothing less than a coup using the Magick at his disposal, and unless we act soon he will be utterly unstoppable!"

"I understand that but I'm afraid my brother would need more in the way of proof."

"He'll have proof enough when the country is in ruins and the devil is abroad!"

"My brother is like me in that he doesn't altogether believe in the devil."

"It matters not one jot," said Crowley, angry, "because the devil believes in you."

"How flattering," said Holmes with a smile. "Forgive me Mr Crowley, we will, of course, do everything we can and let us hope that they can be convinced."

Crowley nodded. "Oh they'll be convinced all right. If my suspicions are right we shall know for sure by midnight tomorrow."

"Midnight?"

"The beginning of the new century Mr Holmes! A potent date indeed. If I know Mathers then that is when his plans will come to fruition. He will wish to claim the twentieth century in the name of Magick!"

After their heated exchange, Crowley, ever the gentleman, became the perfect host of the day before. He roused the others from their beds and my cold collation was exchanged for a full dinner.

Due to the lateness with which we had all arisen, it was already getting dark by the time we began to eat and it was accepted that, however short time may be, there was little we could do for that day.

I feared another attack from Mathers but Crowley seemed to think this unlikely, believing that our enemy would not risk another drain on his powers so close to the execution of his plans. All would be reserved for a a final showdown, he assured me, and that we would do well to learn from Mathers' example and take the time to gather strength. In the morning we would make our way to Inverness and, from there, to London, in the hope that we could intercept Mathers' plan before the suspected hour.

I expected the others to join Crowley in his insistence that Holmes rally the support of Scotland Yard and those he knew within the so-called Corridors of Power. However, perhaps sensing that he was not a man to change his mind readily, they resisted. Crowley, no longer the exasperated fellow of earlier, simply sipped at his wine and assured Holmes that come tomorrow night nobody would be in any doubt as to the threat. His only hope was that between us we would have the power to avert the worst.

I was fascinated to watch Holmes discuss the supernatural. His attitude certainly seemed to have changed. While he was still sceptical, he had the air of someone who may yet believe. He enquired about the principles of what each man did, the different ways in which they fought similar threats. His was the enthusiasm of someone who has discovered a new science and wishes to know more. An analogy which Carnacki certainly shared:

"It is nothing more than a warped branch of physics," he insisted, "and I have no doubt that in the years to come it will be embraced just as the many advances of recent years have been."

"We will accept the existence of ghosts just as we accept the light that comes from electric bulbs or the telephony messages we send over the wires," said Holmes.

"Exactly!" Carnacki declared.

"I cannot agree," said Silence, "these are ancient arts that we have forgotten, not skills of the future. Mankind should be in less of a rush to progress, for what it leaves behind while running blindly towards the future is a loss it will not live long enough to regret."

"True," said Karswell, "all I know I gleaned from research, from the study of the past."

"But with that knowledge you are creating new ideas for the future, no?" Carnacki believed strongly in his subject. "Take my Electric Pentacle, even the revolver with rounds of rock salt and silver."

"Old ideas given a new veneer," said Karswell, "nothing more."

"Well," said Crowley, "as much as I am attracted to the modern advances, I am inclined to agree with the others. Magick is old and comes from the heart not the head. It is a system by which we can alter reality using the power in here." He tapped his chest.

"It is a natural creation," added Karswell, "something that rises up from the earth we stand on." He settled back in his chair swirling his port and clearly on the cusp of telling a story.

"I first became aware of its potency as a child," he continued, "walking in the grounds of the estate I now call my home. We have a maze, probably planted centuries ago. A circular design in evergreen, now carved out, but when I first explored it as a child it was an overgrown nightmare of a place. The hedges were too tall and distended into wedges, thick brambles wound through them that would snag at you as you tried to walk past.

"I was forbidden to explore of course – Mother was always a worrier – but I could never resist.

"Then, one day, predictably enough, I got lost, burrowing deeper and deeper into the heart of that terrible jungle. Why it was allowed to get in such a state, I don't know. After father died mother abandoned certain parts of the upkeep. Also, I think she was scared of the place, I would often catch her gazing at it, as if convinced there was something on the other side, pulling its way out slowly and painfully through the tight-packed branches.

"I screamed and screamed for help, all the while trying to find the exit. But I was turned around and instead I found my way to its very centre.

"The plants were surprisingly sparse, and I managed to peel away the brambles and bindweed to spy a central decoration: a stone plinth topped by a celestial globe. The metal was surprisingly hot given that the sun could barely penetrate, and as I dashed my hand back, fearful of it being burned, the globe toppled, the metal no doubt corroded over the years. The globe collided with the plinth and cracked open like an egg. I can still remember the smell of the air that issued from within it, older than God it seemed to me, filled with the scent of burned earth.

"It made me light-headed and I stumbled, rolling into the brambles where I hung suspended by their weight, looking up at the sky and not daring to move. If I struggled I might work myself even deeper and

the thorns were pressed against my face, hands and legs; if I moved would it not encourage them to break the skin? To my childish mind I feared that once they had got a taste for me, they might not stop.

"I shouted, convinced that sooner or later someone must hear, if not my mother then the groundsman.

"Slowly, above me, the sky began to darken and I knew the shadows of the trees around me would be lengthening. I wondered what might fill those shadows. I knew. Absolutely *knew*, that were I still bound in those brambles – suspended between the earth and that fast-moving sky – when it became utterly dark then I would find out. Because the light was the only thing keeping those creatures away. They were animals of night and shadow and the sun would burn them. And I knew that, unless I was rescued before the darkness came, there would be no boy to find by the morning. I would have been lost, pulled into the damp drifts of pine needles to rot.

"So I reached out with my mind, imagining the scent of that old air that had been released from the celestial sphere. I was charged by the ancient and mystical qualities I knew it must have possessed to have sat there so long. I let it fill me, possess me. And I called! Projected my need for help as if it were the biggest scream the world had ever heard, as if it would have shaken the entire house to its foundations.

"And soon," he said with a smile, "they *came*. I heard both my mother and Perkins the groundsman crashing through the undergrowth like elephants. I called to them then and soon I was being cut free and lifted up in Perkins' great arms, strong with the smell of sweat and soil.

"My mother wanted to have the entire maze cut down but I wouldn't let her. The maze had shown me its secret that day and offered me my first taste of magic.

"I keep it well trimmed now, and often sit at the centre, still marked by that stone plinth and its toppled, cracked sphere. I have never moved them, nor allowed them to be moved. It is my sanctuary, the place where all my magic is born."

There was a moment of silence as we absorbed Karswell's tale. Then Holmes spoke: "It is about conviction too," he said, "is it not? You were certain that your voice would be heard and when they found you, you had no doubt as to how they had done so."

"Belief is key," Crowley agreed, "on both sides."

"Both sides?"

"Belief on the part of the person casting the spell and belief on the person at the receiving end of it. Belief is power, the more you believe in the efficacy of what you do the greater its effect will actually be."

"So magic is not a practice for the insecure?" Holmes asked.

"On the contrary," Carnacki said tactlessly, "I would say that it's a common personalty trait amongst many robe wearers and incense chuckers!"

The look of disdain which Crowley offered Carnacki was almost tangible enough to be shared out as an extra food course. "You have a singular lack of respect for something you appear to have dedicated your life to," he observed.

"I have no interest in practicing magic for the sake of self-development," Carnacki replied, "for that I have cookery. I study magic so that I know how to defend people who need it. If the practicing of magic were banned tomorrow I wouldn't shed a tear, though I'd probably grow rather fat."

Holmes laughed and clapped his hands, then suddenly exchanged his look of glee for one of remonstration when he judged the mood of the room.

"Let's hope your studies are up to scratch then," Crowley said to Carnacki, "for tomorrow you will have the fight of your life."

Over brandy and cigars the scrying ritual was begun. Holmes and I stood well back, allowing Crowley to take centre stage – a position he was clearly accustomed to.

The ritual seemed to involve the use of a map, a couple of crystals and a pendulum made from heavy golden chain. Crowley placed the crystals at the top and bottom of the map, allegedly to focus their energies over the area we were concerned with. The pendulum was then suspended over central London. Crowley closed his eyes and, slowly, the chain began to revolve. After a few moments it came to a halt over a particular spot on the map. At this point, Crowley would check the position then replace the map, using a greater and greater scale so that he could pinpoint the location with accuracy.

"All magic has a signature," Silence explained to Holmes and I at a whisper while Crowley worked. "Like any art, the work can be related to the artist by recognising their styles and signature. Crowley is isolating Mathers' signature – most particularly with reference to the events of last night – and searching for the greatest concentrated traces of that signature within the city."

"Surely that would be the temple of the Golden Dawn?" Holmes asked. "If any building in the city is dripping with the residue of magic, it must be there."

"True," said Silence, "but the trace also fades over time. Mathers will be working somewhere that he knows to be safe and also central to whatever demonstration or attack he has in mind. He will be there now, preparing for whatever rituals he intends to conclude at midnight tomorrow. He knows we'll be looking for him so it will be somewhere hidden."

Holmes nodded.

We didn't have to wait long, Crowley was soon convinced of where we would find Mathers.

"Tottenham Court Road," he announced, folding away the maps.

"Hidden and safe?" asked Holmes with some sarcasm.

"More hidden than you might think," said Crowley, taking a sip of his brandy. "As far as I can tell he is some considerable distance beneath the ground."

"The Underground?" I asked.

"Indeed, Watson," Holmes agreed. "They are working on the new line there are they not?"

"Then that is where he is," said Crowley, "and, one hopes, where he will remain."

CHAPTER TWENTY-TWO

BACK TO THE CAPITAL

At some considerable distress to my confused brain, we arose early the next morning so that we could get to Inverness in time for the first train to the capital. Having struggled to get to sleep in the first place, I found it a cumbersome business waking up. But then nothing makes you so groggy and irritable as to wake up to Holmes smoking his pipe at the foot of your bed.

"Do you mind?" I asked, wafting away great clouds of his foul smoke.

He smiled and left the room, popping his head back through the door a few moments later. "By the way," he said, "don't eat breakfast."

"Why on earth not?" I asked, "I like breakfast!"

"Of course you do," he replied. "It's a meal and you relish those like no other I know. All the same, don't eat or drink anything." He pointed the tip of his pipe at me to emphasise his seriousness. "Nothing at all!" He popped the pipe back in his mouth. "Better not to mention it in front of the others," he said finally. "I'll explain later."

He vanished and I sat up in bed, rubbing the sleep from my eyes and feeling distinctly wretched. What on earth is the point in a morning if there's no bacon in it?

I descended a short while later to the most hateful smell of food wafting from the dining room.

"Come," said Crowley, getting up from his chair, "if we have to travel at this ungodly hour let us at least do so on a full stomach."

"Thank you but no," I replied. "My stomach is somewhat restless first thing."

"Some coffee then?"

"Better not, I'll just make sure I've got everything packed and meet you by the door in, what? Half an hour?"

Crowley looked decidedly crestfallen and I felt bad at rejecting his hospitality, I knew how seriously he took his role as host. "If you're quite sure," he said, "we shall see you then."

I was back downstairs early. It had been the matter of moments to collect my belongings and I decided it would be more pleasant to await the others outside than pacing up and down in the guest room.

Stood on the front step I drew in several large lungfuls of cool morning air. It might be a poor replacement for kedgeree or eggs but it did at least help me to wake up.

As there were so many of us, Charles the coachman had been forced to draft in the assistance of his brother, a surly figure who sat in silence in the driver's seat of a second carriage.

One by one we piled our bags on the back of each vehicle and split up so that Holmes, myself and Crowley went in one carriage while

Carnacki, Silence and Karswell availed themselves of the other.

The journey from Boleskine to Inverness was as lengthy as before and the snow-covered hills and glistening surface of the loch still cast a gloomy countenance around us. For all that, the journey seemed more charged and positive for we were now on the hunt, returning to London in force and with a plan – well, certainly an intent – to take the fight to the opposition.

Crowley was also a more chatty companion than the others had been a day ago. As we passed by he would point out sights of beauty, hills he had climbed, footpaths he had followed. His love for the area was clear, though from his conversation I couldn't imagine him spending the rest of his years at Boleskine, he was clearly a man who would always love to travel. A man who relished the potential of regularly waking up to a brand-new horizon.

Holmes listened politely – or at least appeared to listen, I had no doubt his thoughts circled elsewhere – but didn't really contribute. He and Crowley took a pipe together at one point and then, true to form, my colleague came to life. Murder, tobacco and violent music, these are the subjects upon which Holmes could always be relied upon to expand. Oh, and himself of course. That was probably his favourite subject of all.

By the time Inverness Castle came into view, I was aching and hungry and relieved to be able to climb out of the carriage and stretch my limbs.

The respite was short-lived because we had lost time on our journey and had to run in order to catch our train.

We all gathered in one compartment which would have been perfectly comfortable were it only our bodies it needed to accommodate. Given the size of some of the personalities amongst the group, however, it soon became a little oppressive and I started to wonder how on earth one might survive the hours to come. Carnacki and Crowley were arguing ethics, Holmes and Karswell clashed on several trifling points of genealogy, and Silence and I did our best to stay clear, sat by the corridor as we were.

"To think," I said to him, "had you never visited Baker Street, there never would have been such a meeting of minds."

"The world would have been a more peaceful place, certainly." He gave a small smile and I realised quite how exhausted he looked. Ever since that first morning at Unsworth Guest House he had looked sorely in need of rest; this was a more active lifestyle than the one he was used to. I suggested as much.

"I suppose you're right," he admitted. "I have a little place on Reeves Mews, just along from Hyde Park. I am often so content there, within my library reading with the warm body of Smoke on my lap, that I rarely see the need for all this dashing around. I fear my travelling days are probably done, I have finally found the pleasure in simply staying still."

I talked of my time in Afghanistan – ask any old soldier and he will admit that it never takes him long to bring up war, however much he may claim to not like talking about it – and how difficult I had found it to acclimatise to life in London. How embroiling myself in the early career of Holmes had proved a valuable way of keeping the adrenalin flowing, allowing me to take my place back in society but never quite leaving the battlefield behind. He asked about Mary and there I will admit to faltering.

Holmes and I have lived a great deal of our lives within the public eye, for which I can take the sole blame. After all, I didn't have to publish my accounts of our time together. Still, there were times when I found the scrutiny difficult, none more so than when it came to

Mary's death. It has always been a subject I have skirted over. Indeed, many times I have attempted to avoid it altogether by suggesting that I am in fact still married – a sloppy tactic and one that does a disservice to my readers. A tale means little if you cannot trust the teller. The unreliable narrator... is that what I have let myself become? Perhaps. But I have always had the interests of either my readers (and their wish to be excited) or myself (and the need to keep one thing private) at heart.

I loved her you see, so very much. And it's all very well to re-enact these many moments of high drama on the page, the chases and the gun fights, the clever deductions and the twisted machinations of those that sought to fool Holmes. These are things worthy of turning into words, of immortalising as story. But I will not do that to Mary. I will not turn those last moments of hers – of *ours* – into something constructed to excite or sadden; I will not turn her into fiction.

So forgive me. Mary died. That is that.

I changed the subject and Silence was too much a gentleman to press the matter.

After a few hours, talk led to lunch and a mass exodus was set in motion that would lead us to the dining carriage. At the last moment, however, Holmes took my arm.

"Ah," he said, "if none of you gentlemen object I really could do with a few minutes alone with Watson to discuss matters involved with a previous case. Why don't you eat and we'll chat in your absence?"

"Don't be silly," said Crowley, "talk over lunch, we would love to hear of your business!"

"Client confidentiality," Holmes said, apologetically, "as foolish as it may seem, given what awaits us in the capital, the affair of the duchesses and the poodle really cannot be discussed in an open dining carriage."

He closed the door behind them, giving the men little choice but to progress towards the dining carriage without us.

"I say, Holmes!" I was losing patience with him by now. "What is all this about? The duchesses and the poodle indeed. You sound like a music hall routine."

He began to sing. "Daisy, Daisy, give me your answer do..."

I cuffed him on the arm. "Let's have none of that, things are miserable enough without my having to tolerate your singing. What's going on? What is so private that it couldn't be discussed in front of the others?"

"They have their battle to prepare for," he said, "and we have ours. There can be no doubt that we will fight on different fronts." He smiled. "Beyond the odd bit of sleight of hand I am no magician, but to do so I need to plan. Do you have paper?"

"Of course, my notebook is in my bag."

"Excellent, then fetch it and let us construct a map of the Underground."

"A map?" I sighed. "I really don't think I know it well enough to do so."

"You know it better than I. Together we shall try."

And we did, though the last of it was finished by Silence and Carnacki who, having returned from their lunch, were only too happy to help.

"There," I said, following the routes with my finger, "though why it is so important I don't know."

Looking up at Holmes I was infuriated to find he'd fallen asleep.

He really could be the most damnable man.

Given the length of our journey it was already late in the afternoon by the time we arrived at St Pancras and we immediately hailed two cabs to take us all to the building site on the junction of Oxford Street and Tottenham Court Road.

Even in the late afternoon the traffic was thick. Cabs and carts trotted along in both directions over several lanes, the roar of the pedestrians, one hundred conversations rolled into one massive wall of sound. Could all of this, all of these people with their busy lives, really be in danger?

We looked at the large barricades that surrounded the excavation.

"Would it not be better to get some assistance?" I asked.

"I'm afraid even I would need more evidence to convince the great and good to come down here just yet," Holmes replied.

"Evidence," sighed Crowley, "while the soul of the world hangs in the balance."

Holmes looked as though he was about to argue when a terrible explosion tore through the noise of the crowds. As one we turned to see a plume of smoke rising from further up the street.

"What the devil?" I strained to see what had happened, my instincts as a doctor driving me towards where I might be needed. A hand on my shoulder – that of Silence – stopped me.

"Wait," he said. "Look..."

And as he spoke I became aware of the sound of a wind blowing its way towards us, that high-pitched scream of a storm forcing its way between buildings. A wind that sung.

Looking down Oxford Street, the smoke from the explosion bent towards us and then simply vanished, dissipated through the air. Carts blew upwards, spinning on the tornado's back; people screamed, horses stampeded.

The wind moved in a casual, almost lethargic manner, swaying from one side of the street to the other. Sending shop signs spinning and awnings flapping skywards.

But before the wind, becoming more and more discernible as their numbers increased, a group of people began to advance towards us. A handful became a crowd, a crowd became a mob... More and more joined the throng. Some were clearly wounded, rivulets of blood trickling down slack-jawed faces, limbs askew, feet dragging. But nothing seemed to stop them, an ever-increasing wave of people staring, screaming, seemingly meaninglessly, at the air.

"Dear God," said Carnacki, "I have heard of them, soldiers who claimed they were used as cannon fodder by the Wassoulou Empire, explorers who say they have seen them created through the power of Voudou... *nzumbe!*"

"What?"

Carnacki looked at me and for the very first time I could tell he was afraid. "The walking dead!"

CHAPTER TWENTY-THREE

THE BREATH OF GOD

"We need to get below ground before it reaches us," Silence shouted above the noise of the approaching storm. "Quickly!"

We needed no further encouragement. Carnacki hunched over the padlock that secured a length of chain holding the workmen's barrier closed. Within seconds there was a jangle of chain and he pulled the tall wooden barricade back far enough for us all to enter. Once we had all run inside, Carnacki yanked the chain tight, relocked it, and we all dashed ahead into the darkness.

There was a flash of light as Crowley lit one of a string of lanterns left hanging from a pole at the entrance of the pit. He passed it to Karswell and lit a couple more.

Behind us the work barrier rocked in its frame and the noise was that of a giant knocking on the very doors of Hell.

A set of rough steps were cut into the earth, shored up by stones and wooden props, and we descended even further, the lights of the lanterns reminding us of how enclosed the space was around us.

Soon we could tell that there was light ahead and we extinguished our own lanterns, not wishing to advertise our presence.

"It must be Mathers," I said, glancing to Holmes for confirmation. My friend remained silent, his face slack and impassive. I realised he hadn't said a word since the explosion above ground. Was he in shock? For all his pretence of giving the supernatural credence, was the sight of it now more than his logical mind had been ready for?

"Holmes?" I whispered, not wanting to cause him embarrassment in front of the others. "Are you all right?"

He looked at me and his big, dark eyes were as haunting as the tunnel we were in.

"Dear God, John," he whispered, "I only hope you will forgive me."

"Don't be ridiculous," I said. "It's a lot to take in. Of course I forgive you!"

I had completely misunderstood what he was trying to say, but I wouldn't know that until later.

The tunnel opened out onto what would clearly soon be the train platform and, for all our intent of sneaking up on whoever was down here, a cry erupted from the far end of the platform, where a peculiarly plain, rectangular train engine stood.

"'Ere," called the voice, "who goes there, then?"

Carnacki was quick to take the lead, pulling his revolver from his pocket and aiming it at the man. "I might ask you the same question," he replied.

"You might," said the man coldly, "but as I'm *supposed* to be down here, minding the company business, I still say you're the ones with explaining to do."

"You're here alone?" Carnacki asked.

"Running 'er up to Bank ain't I?" he said, gesturing towards the train. "Checking how she goes. The navvies are away home. 'Ere," he gestured towards the gun, "no need for that is there? I ain't going to be getting in your way. Don't want no trouble."

Crowley turned to the rest of us. "We could use the train!" he said. "Travel to the interchange at Bank. From there we can plan our defence." He appealed directly to Holmes. "We might just be able to hold them off long enough for you to contact the government and draft in reinforcements."

"Who knows how quickly its influence will spread?" Karswell said. "Half of London could be gone by the time we get there."

"All the more reason to move quickly!" Crowley insisted, turning and addressing the train driver. "There has been a terrible accident above ground," he said, "we need you to take us to Bank with you so we can alert the authorities."

The driver nodded and suddenly I experienced a strange, dislocating feeling, I looked at the man's face and I caught a whiff of the ocean.

"Room for all of you onboard," he said, "I've got a single carriage linked up." He climbed into the driver's compartment and flipped a couple of heavy switches. There was a hum as the electrical current began to flow through the circuit and the train moved forward to reveal the carriage behind. The driver cut the power once more. "Jump aboard!" he shouted and the momentary feeling that had washed over me ebbed away.

We all climbed in and, once we were seated, that hum returned and the train began to move along the tunnel.

I imagine the sensation is entirely lost now, but at that time electric trains were a thing of the future. Within six months the Central

London Railway would be up and running, and the "twopenny tube" would be so popular that the novelty would soon wear off. That day, however, it was yet another piece of magic amongst so much else.

I sat down and looked to each of my fellow passengers.

Carnacki was clearly as charged as the metal track beneath us: he refused to sit down, keeping his gun in his hand and pacing up and down.

"I say," Karswell said to him, proffering up a small bundle. "Your lock-picking paraphernalia," he smiled, "you dropped it when breaking into the station so masterfully."

Carnacki looked at him in confusion for a moment. Then took the wrapped lock-picks and dropped them into his pocket. "Thank you," he said and resumed his pacing. Karswell shrugged and took a seat, surprisingly calm.

Crowley was also remarkably relaxed given our situation. It occurred to me that, with matters finally come to a climax, he was able to tackle things head on rather than second-guessing what Mathers intended. I had seen such a calm dedication descend on Holmes in the past, when all the mystery was gone and all that lay ahead was resolution.

That was not my colleague's current mood, however; his eyes were darting from one part of the carriage to another, that wonderful brain of his adding data like an accountant's counting machine.

Silence was not relaxed either, in fact his brow glistened with sweat and he looked close to breaking down. I assumed that the pressure was finally beginning to take its toll.

"What have you done?" someone asked, and for a moment I had no idea who it was, the voice was so quiet, barely audible above the hum of the electrics.

"What have you done?" Holmes asked again, looking up towards Crowley with such rage in his eyes that I confess I felt afraid myself. "And by my delayed action what have I allowed to happen?"

"What do you mean?" Crowley asked. "I'm just doing the best I can to save our necks." His face was a perfect mask of indignation. "And as many others as possible, naturally. Mathers must hope that..."

"Oh shut up!" Holmes roared, slamming the ferrule of his cane against the floor of the carriage. "Mr Samuel Liddell MacGregor Mathers has not the slightest connection to this case and never had!"

"But surely —" I began, only for a look from Holmes to stop the words in my throat.

"This has always been *you*, Crowley," Holmes continued, "and Silence," he added, sparing an acidic glance towards the guilty-looking doctor, "and Karswell." His last look was for Carnacki. "I confess the only person I was unsure about was you, but you're as innocent in all this as Watson and I, aren't you?"

"What are you talking about man?" Carnacki demanded.

"Pay attention and I will tell you," Holmes replied, "though might I ask that you point that gun towards our fellows? I have no wish for them to interrupt."

"If you think I'm going to let you just slander our names without interruption..." began Crowley.

But Silence was quick to speak this time. "Do as he says Aleister, and shut up. This has gone much too far."

"Indeed it has," agreed Holmes, "much too far."

Crowley appeared on the cusp of arguing once more but then, unbelievably, his face broke out in a smile. "Very well," he said, "you can have your moment, after all it's much too late for you to do anything about it, even if you had proof, which I very much doubt."

"I have none whatsoever," Holmes agreed, reaching into his pocket for his cigarette case. He never could explain himself without a cigarette in his hand. My friend was such an absurd creature of habit. "But I will tell you what I know, nonetheless."

CHAPTER TWENTY-FOUR

THE LAST SIGH

"From the first it was exceedingly suspicious," he said, lighting his cigarette and exhaling a mouthful of smoke. "Why was the good Doctor John Silence on our doorstep? And in so uncharacteristic a state of untidiness? He hadn't rushed to see us after the bizarre events he described, that much was clear both from his story and the fact that his legs were coated with the hair of his dog. He had come straight from his home in..." He looked to Silence. "I believe you told Watson it was on Reeves Mews?"

"It is."

"Just the other side of Grosvenor Square. I take it that De Montfort was running to you for aid when he died?"

Silence nodded.

"Aid he would not have received," Holmes continued, "but let us keep these matters in their proper order, they are complex enough without jumbling them up.

"The only other reason we can imagine you were walking around in such an unconventional state from your norm is that you were distracted, alarmed, worried. Not yourself in other words. What could be agitating you so? Surely not the details of your story, if your reputation is to be believed then the possessed and the phantasmagorical is your very bread and butter. Such matters – alarming as they may be to others – could hardly be thought of as a divergence from your usual routine. And yet, something clearly bothered you. Was it perhaps something so simple as your meeting with me? Something you *had* to do? Something that sat uncomfortably?"

"I have never been comfortable with this business," admitted Silence, "but I was doing what I thought was right."

"That excuse has been given for many atrocities over the years," said Holmes. "Of course not a single word of your story was true, it existed solely to engage my curiosity, to get me involved. What other reason could there have been for your visit if we assume – as I began to do – that your intentions were not altogether honourable? At the time such an idea was supposition. It was simply the only logical reason *if* we come at matters from the assumption that you were a liar."

"As a cynic always would," I said.

"Indeed," Holmes replied. "I said to you on the train that you must be willing to believe didn't I? Yet a good deal of my deduction started from entirely the opposite viewpoint: if one assumed that *none* of what I was being led to believe was possible, what explanation could be found to explain the facts? It really is the only way to deduce anything. Assume everything is false until you cannot explain it any other way."

"You're saying this is all fabrication?" Carnacki asked. "What about everything we've seen?"

"Oh there is *something* out there," Holmes said, "some kind of force that we may as well label as 'supernatural' for certainly we do not currently have the ability to explain it. Though I must admit," he smiled at Carnacki, "I find your attitude – that all of this is merely science of the future – much easier to accept than the archaic superstition of your fellows.

"Anyway," he continued, "let us not get side tracked. I have explained the position with which I approached everything. And from that perspective what do we actually know? Silence told us a story that is not a matter of facts, it is merely a ghoulish tale he wished us to believe. Likewise Crowley's saga of supernatural attacks, they were no more genuine than his affectation of being a Scottish laird. They simply didn't happen."

"But what about what I saw then?" I asked, my mind reeling from all of this. "That was no lie."

"My dear friend," said Holmes, "it may not have been a lie but it most certainly was an exaggeration.

"It is all about belief. You explained that much to me last night, Crowley. And that, at least, helped explain the discrepancy between the deaths of Hilary De Montfort and Lord Ruthvney.

"De Montfort's death was most convincing: bruises that were almost impossible to explain, apparently the result of a supernatural force. A force that Silence was at pains to tell us was the Breath of God.

"And then we travel to the country and see the scene of the crime at Ruthvney Hall. Again, there is plenty of evidence of a supernatural storm. And yet he was poisoned. Sent mad – just as Watson suggested – by a gas introduced into the room via his smoking chimney.

"Gentlemen, one has to wonder, if the very wrath of God is marching around the Home Counties, why it was necessary for Ruthvney to be killed in such a colourful, yet ultimately earthly manner. It didn't make sense. So it was, once again, suspicious.

"On our walk in the grounds we find evidence of three people involved. Well that is useful, we know we're looking for multiple assassins at least. One of whom lives up to the name by smoking a mix of tobacco and hashish." He looked to Crowley. "You emptied your tobacco out on arrival at Ruthvney Hall and I can assure you that, had I not recognised it then, I most certainly would have done during our conversation in the coach earlier."

I remembered Holmes and Crowley discussing each other's tobacco during the journey to Inverness. Typical of Holmes, he rarely makes small talk without good reason.

"We also find a ring, a pentacle in onyx with the inscription 'To S.L.M.M.' inside. A most unsubtle clue, gentlemen. Am I to accept that my enemy is wandering around the woods at night with ill-fitting jewellery? We were always supposed to find it, of course, or rather I was, because it served one other purpose." He looked to me. "When you picked up the ring what happened to you?"

"Well, I snagged my arm on the brambles," I said, "it was hard not to, they were so thick."

"Hard not to, indeed," Holmes agreed, "and thus you took the first dose of a chemical agent that has been affecting your judgement ever since. It's no coincidence that you hallucinated shortly afterwards, no coincidence at all."

"I was poisoned?"

"Indeed, precisely why I have been keeping you away from any food or drink for the day, a singularly difficult task in your case.

"That was your first dose. Your second came from the newspaper vendor who so generously shared his rum with you,"

"The driver!" I shouted, pointing towards the head of the train. "I knew I recognised him!"

"An employee of Mr Crowley in fact," Holmes said, "a fourth member of their gang."

"Then on the train to Inverness?" I asked. "Surely we all saw something?"

"Well," said Holmes "you *experienced* something, that's for sure, every passenger in the restaurant carriage did. But again the food was poisoned, just as every morsel you ate at Crowley's would have been." He looked to Crowley. "I assume you were onboard the train?" Crowley nodded, a calm smile still in place. "Then you should have made a point of poisoning my veal," Holmes said, returning the smile, "had you done so I might not have been able to retain the clear-minded perspective from which all my deductions have grown."

Behind Holmes the tunnel opened out into British Museum Station, lamps hanging around the nearly completed platform. In the sudden burst of light, I noticed at the rear of the train there was another carriage, wrapped tightly in tarpaulins. What were we carrying?

"I say again –" Holmes leaned forward in his seat – "I don't for one minute claim that there is nothing unusual at work here, I may be a rationalist but that doesn't mean I'm an idiot. There are powers at work that are beyond my reasoning, beyond my *understanding*... but those powers have been exaggerated and every encounter with them stage-managed. Why? Because of something I *do* understand: greed.

"That's what this has been about. This extended horror show, from the first death to that unholy act of terrorism on Oxford Street. All of it designed to make three people appear important, our future saviours, the masterful magicians: Aleister Crowley, Julian Karswell and Dr Silence."

"No," Silence insisted, "it wasn't as petty as that. Civilisation is moving too fast! It's forgetting all the powers and spirituality of the past. We needed to remind them, to make them remember what true power is, to relearn the lessons they have forgotten. We needed them to be afraid."

"And, of course, the more people who believe how powerful you are, how powerful *it* is –" Holmes gestured out of the carriage window into the darkness outside – "the more powerful you all become. Because that's how it works, isn't it? Belief is key? Yes? On both sides?"

"Hilary De Montfort believed didn't he? And look how effective the Hellish wind was on him.

"Lord Ruthvney? Not so much, he was no occultist, sufficient digging by Langdale Pike was enough to confirm that. He was just a major shareholder in the line upon which we are currently travelling. I presume you wanted his papers? Forge authorisation for you to work here?"

"We needed his authorisation to have this train laid on for our use," Silence said, "they weren't planning on running anything along the tracks for months yet."

Holmes nodded. "And once that was organised another death, particularly one as absurd as that, all helps the theatre doesn't it? Keeps me involved, excites the readers of the popular press, has them eagerly awaiting the next grisly happening."

"But why involve you at all?" I asked Holmes.

"We said it ourselves at the very outset of this case," he replied, "I have become the detective who is known for solving the impossible. I would have become involved anyway. All the better if I was involved under their *control*, guided into accepting their side of the story. Then of course – as they have so frequently requested – I would endorse their actions with Scotland Yard and indeed the government. The word of Holmes? The most famous rationalist in the country? What better endorsement could they have!

"The only thing I don't understand," he admitted, "is why you involved Carnacki. I know it was Karswell who hired him, the stench of his outdoor temple, the yew tree and the verdigris sculpture gave that away." He looked to Carnacki. "Congratulations on both the precision of your memory and the sharpness of your senses by the way, you're almost to my standard."

"Too kind," Carnacki replied.

"But wasn't he too much of a risk?" Holmes continued. "Someone who might see through what you were up to?"

"That was Karswell's fault," Crowley said. "I must admit I thought it was over-egging the pudding somewhat but he was convinced that if we could fool you then Carnacki would be no problem. And what harm could there be in one more recommendation? He is rather well thought of by a number of landed gentry, after all."

"I've exorcised enough of them," Carnacki said, "but surely there was more to it than that?"

"I hoped you might introduce me to your friend, the writer, Dodgson," Karswell admitted, "with his connections at *The Idler* magazine I thought he might have helped me find a publisher."

Holmes actually laughed at that. "Unbelievable," he said. "You construct that entire shadowplay just to entice someone who may be able to help you get in print? Unearthly creatures appearing within the bookstacks! You killed a publisher doing so!"

"He'd already turned the manuscript down," Karswell said with a shrug, "a short-sightedness he lived long enough to regret as I fed it to him, page by brilliant page."

Holmes sneered in disgust. "You petty little man."

"Don't you dare call me that or I swear you'll regret it!" Karswell shouted, pointing menacingly at Holmes. "Nobody insults me and lives!"

"I've been threatened by much worse than pathetic little bookworms like you," Holmes said dismissively. "Now," he looked to me and Carnacki, "the chemical that they have been poisoning you both with, as well as gassing the poor survivors of the bomb explosion above..."

"The *nzembe*," Carnacki said.

Holmes nodded. "Nothing of the sort, just hallucinating victims, more theatre, briefly glimpsed, to build up to their grand final act."

"Which is?" I asked.

Holmes nodded towards the rear of the carriage. "You'll notice we're pulling a freight container. I imagine it holds more of the gas we saw used above."

Silence nodded. "I synthesised it myself. You've seen the sort of hallucinations it can cause."

"Indeed. Am I right in thinking you plan to release it at Bank?"

Silence nodded again. "From there you can access the entire Underground, the gas would float up all over the city, contaminate thousands."

"Mass murder," Holmes said. "I hope your conscience burns, Doctor."

"The gas doesn't kill," Silence insisted, "Watson's proof of that. But the things they'll see!"

"Enough to convince anyone of angels and demons." I said.

"Precisely," Silence agreed, "and with the whole city convinced of the supernatural, we will come into our own, happy to save their lives and souls and bring society back to a more cautious, spiritual level. What we're doing is for the benefit of mankind, however it may appear to the contrary."

"The gas was enough to kill Ruthvney," Holmes argued, "driven to grotesque suicide by his visions. Many more will die as you subject the capital to your brutal empire of fear. Kindly don't attempt to hold any moral high ground Silence, your hands are as bloody as those of your fellows. But no matter, we shall see the gas is never released."

"Oh, I don't know," Crowley said. "I don't think we've quite run out of options yet. I haven't been entirely idle while Holmes has been preaching from his pulpit."

Light suddenly burst through the windows as we appeared at Chancery Lane Station and Crowley's face bore a terrifying rictus of ill humour. "I have summoned our faithful servant to once again assist in our efforts."

The train bucked violently as that terrifying force, the so-called Breath of God, hit us from the rear. Carnacki toppled forward, the gun falling from his hands. The train's metal wheels screeched on the rails as the driver hit the brakes. For a moment all was chaos. Holmes rebounded off the wall, Crowley reaching for his throat. Silence held his head in his hands and rolled along the floor towards the driver. I was pressed back in my seat, reaching out for Carnacki in the hope that I could help break his fall. Karswell did the best of us all, he jumped for the gun.

"No!" Silence cried, lying on his back by the front exit. "This has gone too far!"

Karswell pointed the gun and fired, shooting Silence right between the eyes.

"Nobody tells me what to do!" Karswell shouted. "Nobody!" He turned the gun towards Carnacki but the younger man was already on the move.

"Quickly, Doctor!" he yelled, flinging Holmes' dropped cane at Karswell. "The door!"

The tip of the cane jabbed Karswell in the face and his hands went up with a startled cry. His clenched fingers pulled the trigger and a bullet went into the roof of the carriage, sending out a shower of wood splinters and dust. Taking the moment of grace offered, I opened the door closest to me and both Carnacki and I toppled out onto the platform.

The wind was still curling around the walls of the station, sending the various cables and posters flapping against the tiles or whipping around our heads.

"We need to keep moving," Carnacki shouted over the noise. "Come on!"

"But Holmes!"

I turned back to see him through the carriage window wrestling with Crowley. I also saw Karswell raising the gun to fire once more.

"Duck!" Carnacki cried. We both ran up the platform towards the exit. Two bullets ricocheted off the tunnel wall sending fragments of tile and plaster tumbling into our hair.

The exit was sealed, no escape that way.

"The track," said Carnacki, snatching a lantern, "no other choice."

He pulled me past the front of the train. Through the window I saw that duplicitous old sailor cowering from the threat of gunfire. Carnacki aimed towards the edge of the platform. "Careful!" I warned him, yanking him back. "The central rail is electrified."

We slipped down as carefully as we could and ran ahead into the darkness, the sound of the wind growing louder and louder behind us.

"We can't possibly outrun it!" said Carnacki, passing me the lantern. "Our only chance is to fight it."

He removed his cufflinks, kissed them tenderly then turned and threw them into the tunnel behind us, muttering an incantation under his breath as he did so. In the low light it was impossible to tell precisely what was happening, but a shimmer of light passed across the whole tunnel as if a firework had been ignited in our wake. There was a deep bellowing sound that I could only imagine was the Breath of God colliding with some form of barrier, though there was nothing I could see.

"Keep moving!" Carnacki insisted. "I don't know how long that will hold."

My ears had popped as if something had sucked the air out of the tunnel and I massaged them as we ran, trying to get my hearing to return. Slowly they cleared, in time to hear the thing I had feared, that dull hum of electric current. Crowley had gained control once more.

"The train's coming!" I said. "It'll mow us down!" Then a thought occurred to me. "Or pick us up."

I turned and flung my lantern at the wall where it exploded sending a trail of frame licking across the dirty brick.

"What are you doing?" Carnacki asked.

There was no time to explain. As I had hoped the electric sound shifted in pitch, as the driver – that fraudulent old soak – panicked at the sudden explosion and slowed the train's engine, uncertain what he was driving into.

"Jump on!" I said, and we ran back towards the train, clambering onto the slight scoop at the front. Gripping the edge of the windows, on either side of the driver, we could hang there, somewhat precariously, as the train once again picked up speed and moved along the tunnel.

"All he can do is hope we fall off!" I called, looking up at the infuriated face of the driver.

"An objective he may yet see fulfilled," Carnacki replied, gritting his teeth and trying to work the tips of his fingers more firmly into their holds.

The train began to speed up and it was all we could do to maintain our grip.

"We might be able to jump clear at the next station?" I suggested.

"One of us may," Carnacki agreed. "It rather depends what side of the train the platform is on."

I saw what he meant. While it was certainly in the realms of possibility for whichever of us was on the same side as the platform, there would not be time for the other to inch across the front of the train in order to jump.

"Then let's both be ready," I said, "so we can take the chance when it's offered."

Both of us hung there, trying to twist our heads so that we could see ahead and anticipate our chances. Soon, light appeared.

"Your side," Carnacki said and I felt bad for him as he tried to shift his grip before it slipped. "Best of luck."

I dropped my body weight to my left, the opposite direction to the platform, waiting for the right moment. I would need to swing myself, using momentum to jump in the right direction. Hopefully the wind resistance, pushing past the nose of the train, should help carry me. The train's speed was limited, fast enough to offer a genuine threat of injury but slow enough that I might just manage the manoeuvre with my legs intact. There was only one way to find out. I tensed and then flung myself towards the light and the platform beyond it. For one terrible second it was all in the air – would I make it or not? Then I hit the platform and rolled. I got to my feet as quickly as I could and ran back towards the train. Was it long enough? Would I have time?

I jumped towards the final carriage, grabbing at the ropes that held the tarpaulin in place. It was smaller than a passenger carriage and, clambering over the top of the gas canister, I was able to look directly through the rear window and into the carriage we had originally been sat in.

Holmes was up and still fighting, though I could tell from a fast blossoming bruise on his cheek that he had taken something of a beating. He turned towards me and I saw a momentary flicker of recognition on his face as he caught sight of me through the window. He turned his back on me and did his best to block any view of me from the Karswell or Crowley who were at the front of the carriage.

I could only hope that Carnacki had managed to maintain his grip.

I inched forward, wondering whether I might be able to disconnect this last carriage from the rest of the train. But if I raised my head a fraction too far, the roof of the tunnel would shave it right off me.

The sound of raised voices alerted me to trouble. In the carriage Holmes was being shoved out of the way as Karswell ran towards the rear window.

"I knew it!" he shouted. "Crowley! He's here, the bastard's here!"

Karswell yanked down the window and pointed his gun to fire.

"Don't be an idiot man!" Crowley shouted. "You'll hit the gas!"

I didn't know what else to do but duck as the sound of a gunshot rang out. The shot went wide – it would later become clear that Holmes had pushed Karswell to ruin his aim – but there was a popping nose, like a champagne cork, from a foot or so away. It was followed by the hissing sound of escaping gas. He'd breached the canister.

I did my best to hold my breath, sure that the gas must be flooding around me. It was too late though, for the effects of that terrible poison began to make themselves felt. The jolting of the train wheels against the track got louder and louder, like the pounding of a blacksmith's hammer, and I became aware that the tarpaulin was shifting underneath me.

"John..." whispered a voice, still audible over the noise of the wheels, "take my hand John, I'll keep you safe."

As the tarpaulin slipped away it revealed what was left of my wife. The years had been cruel and the fingers that reached for me, tickling my cheek and leaving a little of themselves there, were far thinner than even the dainty hand of the woman I had loved with all my strength.

"Not real," I said, begging myself to believe, even as her other hand pushed its way between the buttons of my shirt and raked my skin with tips too hard and wet to be nails. "Not real!"

"Oh, John," it said, breathless, as if its lungs couldn't hold enough air, punctured and withered like old bellows, "I'll always be real to you."

I screamed, my voice matching the brakes as the train slowed down on approaching Bank. The lights of the station flooded over me, showing something I could not bear to see. I screamed and screamed, tumbling from the canister and onto the platform.

Others began to scream around me and I thought then that it was proof of my visions, but of course the gas was still flowing and the passengers gathered on the other platforms had visions of their own. Perhaps the lights turned into branding irons, hissing their way towards unblemished skin. Maybe worms filled the tunnels ahead of the trains, their blind snouts straining upward towards the stairs and an escape to street level. Maybe, like me, they simply saw the horror of what our loved ones become when we have the terrible burden of outliving them.

In a panic crowds of passengers began running for the stairs, desperate to escape the impossible terrors that surrounded them.

"Watson!" I heard his voice, that fine voice of logic and reason that has pulled me back from many a moment when I have been close to death. For all his irritations, for all I could really *punch* him some days, he has always been there. He has made my life what it is and, for better or worse, I would have no other.

I felt hands grabbing at me and for a moment, I fought them off. It was the sound of a gunshot that brought me to my senses and I realised it was Holmes holding on to me. I looked and saw Karswell racing towards us, the pistol held out in front of him.

"Stick to your books, Karswell," I said, getting to my feet and doing my best to force away the sensation that Mary was still gripping me, clambering on my back and trying to get inside me.

Then I changed my mind. This was *not* my Mary but if it had been, no matter what she looked like, I loved her and if she had been with me, gripping me close, I would have been charged by the experience not scared of it. It would have made me *stronger*.

"Oh," I said, grinning thanks to the newfound strength in my chest, "and my wife says to tell you: learn to count!"

Karswell's fingers squeezed the trigger but he'd had his six shots and I punched him so hard in the jaw that my fingers ached pleasantly for over twenty-four hours afterwards.

Holmes was holding himself up against the wall of the station.

"Are you all right my friend?" I asked.

He looked me right in the eye and the determination he showed was every inch the match for my own. "It takes more than phantasms to stop me, John Watson," he said. "Let's rout these imbeciles once and for all, eh?"

The driver, his nerve broken both by the gas and the impending realisation that it was the gaol for him unless he made himself scarce, was running, screaming along the platform. He dashed up the stairs, beating at something imagined that fluttered around his head.

Carnacki slowly pulled himself onto the platform, his arms shaking from holding on for so long, the gas making his eyes bulge and his mouth shout threats at the air around him. Crowley was stood between us, his long hair awry, his face absurdly happy below engorged pupils. "Yes!" he cried. "This is the world. *This is my world!*"

I have no idea what creatures surrounded him in his hallucinations but the pleasure he took in their presence was terrible to see. As the last few bystanders ran for the surface we were presented with a miniature vision of his proposed future: the lunatic despot luxuriating in the terror of others.

Holmes pushed past him and climbed into the driver's cab. After a few moments the train began to reverse and Holmes jumped back out. Slowly, the train built up speed and vanished from sight, pushing the gas canister ahead of it.

"It'll keep going until reaches the terminus," Holmes said. "Then it will stop somewhat dramatically. The gas should dissipate along the length of the line."

"No!" Crowley shouted. "You will not take my beautiful demons from me!"

There was a screech of wind and suddenly the platform was filled with the Breath of God, chasing round and around the walls, knocking us from our feet and pushing us along the ground. Holmes, Carnacki and I fought our way towards the stairs, crawling from one platform to the other.

"I will have my world!" Crowley shouted, pursuing us relentlessly. "I will!"

Holmes slowly stood up. Against all reason, the wind still blowing just as hard around us.

"No," he said, calmly, "you will not. Because this will be the century of change, the century when the human race forges ahead with the mad vigour it always has. It won't have time for your world, your dark, dark world with its superstitions and fears. With its gods that rage and demand pain and sorrow and blood enough to colour oceans. The human race will finally turn its back on that world, it won't even see it any more, far too busy being blinded by the beautiful, brilliant lights of the future. It won't believe in you, and that's what matters, isn't it?" He was nose to nose with Crowley by now and utterly unruffled by the wind, because for him it didn't blow. "Belief," he said. "Without it you are nothing but a man screaming into the dark."

The wind ceased and Crowley, tears in his eyes, staggered back along the platform. The groaning Karswell had moved across from the other side, confused by the wind and the solid jolt I'd given his dull brain. Crowley grabbed him, tugging him over the side and onto this new stretch of track. "Come on," he said. "We'll have our time, they'll see, we'll have our time."

They disappeared into the tunnel, Crowley's voice echoing back a few moments later.

"Our time is coming!" he screamed. "It's coming!"

"Yes," Holmes said, as the sound of a train whistle filled the air, "as is the nine forty-five to Waterloo." He looked up at me as the sound of Crowley and Karswell screaming echoed back along the tunnel and into the station. "And that, like progress, simply cannot be stopped."

The train pulled up to the platform and, with a macabre grin, Holmes held out his hands beckoning for Carnacki and I to join him.

"We've earned ourselves some dinner," he said, "to see in the New Year!"

Tomorrow would see the horror brought home as the reports came in of how many had been harmed during the two gas attacks. Between the explosion on Oxford Street and the inevitable casualties during the mass exodus of Bank Station, thirty-nine people died, with twice that injured physically and countless more mentally. That was perhaps the worst legacy, those that had been shown the very worst their imaginations could throw at them, forced to live with what they had seen. To think the foolish John Silence could have ever thought that what they were doing was for the betterment of mankind. There's nothing so easily deluded as a man with good intentions.

Holmes, Carnacki and I were desperate to wash the foul events away with celebration. Nothing sharpens the appetite more than near-death.

After a brief stop at Scotland Yard where a confused Inspector Gregson was told all he needed to know for now (Holmes would only too happily discuss the case in minutiae come the morning but for now he wished to walk away from it all; as much as he bemoaned the reputation he laboured under, it did allow him to behave quite outrageously at times). We decamped to one of Holmes' favourite restaurants, a little bistro just off Mayfair.

"It was the most devilish business," I said, once we were surrounded by the detritus of a meal well done. "I still cannot begin to fathom it all."

"You will," Holmes said with a smile, "once you've had another glass of wine."

"I say," Carnacki said, who, for all his snobbery about the menu had enjoyed his meal a great deal, "who was it that tried to shoot me do you think?"

"Silence," Holmes said. "Watson here heard him weeping away in the night, troubled by a guilty conscience. No doubt it had been decided by Crowley that you really were one complication too many. They met shortly after the two of you had retired. I believe you both saw Silence wandering up the street."

"I thought it was you," I admitted.

"Which is why you make an excellent doctor but only a passable detective."

"Silence thought he was doing the right thing," I said. "He was acting according to his beliefs."

"As soon as your belief costs a single innocent life," Holmes said, "you lose the right to hide behind its justification. None of us are above that rule. As all three of them have now learned. Fatally."

Though actually this would turn out not to be the case. While the body of Dr Silence was found just where it should be, amongst the wreckage of their commandeered train, the same could not be said of either Crowley or Karswell.

The former reappeared in America, hiding out in New York where he attempted to make a nominal living as a writer. Certainly, it seemed his grander ambitions had been beaten from him. Holmes, forever determined that he would see the man put to account for his crimes – crimes for which we still had no admissible evidence whatsoever – made a point of following Crowley's movements, ready to pounce should the circumstances allow. It soon became clear that such action would not be necessary. Even now, Crowley makes something of a name for himself as "the wickedest man in the world" – a name given to him by the *Daily Express* newspaper, which, in fairness, doles out such high-handed epithets on an almost daily basis – but he is a spent force. Worshipped by those who are always inclined to worship someone, feared by those who find fear comes easily. But is he believed? No. The majority simply view him as a scandalous rogue, an opinion with which I will not argue. On that terrible night, the cusp of a brand-new age, he had set his sights higher. But the brand-new age really didn't want him, certainly not in sufficient numbers for Holmes to ever be concerned.

As for Karswell, there was some fuss about the publication of his "magnum opus", the somewhat prosaically titled: *History of Witchcraft*. The book was terribly received and Holmes grew concerned that he might have to involve himself when one of the reviewers, a man by the name of Harrington, died in rather mysterious circumstances. In the end there was little with which to concern ourselves, however, and the matter seemed to come to its own satisfactory conclusion.

But all of that was in the future.

On that night, everything seemed all too rich with the possibility of change. I was still trying to decide what was real and what was not. I had experienced so much that simply couldn't be explained away. I did not – and still do not – know what to think.

"Who is to say what our beliefs are now?" I smiled and topped up my glass, just as Holmes had suggested. "So many things to accommodate into our view of the world."

"My views haven't changed," said Holmes. "When you have eliminated the impossible, whatever remains, however improbable, must be the truth."

Notes on What is Real and What is Not
(To be read after the novel)

The Quick Answer: None of it is true.

The Long Answer: A good deal of it is true. With some reservations.

Some Reservations
1. Aleister Crowley

Our main concern is Aleister Crowley, the rest of our characters are fictional and are therefore resilient enough to look after themselves (just as they have for the decades before I got my grubby hands on them). However, it takes very little reading to realise that the public face of Crowley was often as fictional as Holmes, and I therefore have no issue with doing what I like with him. That said, it would be extremely unfair not to point out – for the few that may need it – what is utter fabrication. Crowley very successfully created his own notoriety: he doesn't need my help.

For many years it was de rigeur to paint Crowley as a villain. Indeed, the *Daily Express* did label him – as Watson himself points out – "the wickedest man in the world". This is blatant nonsense, he was contentious, bigoted and perhaps a little mad but he was certainly never truly wicked. Nonetheless he excited a great number of authors, being the inspiration behind such creations as Mocata in Dennis Wheatley's *The Devil Rides Out*, Somerset Maugham's Oliver Haddo and, indeed, Julian Karswell (ahem) in MR James' *Casting the Runes* (but more on him later).

Later biographers redressed the balance, many of them painting him in an extremely positive light as a philosopher and author rather than scoundrel. It is perhaps this renaissance that saw him placed on 2002's "100 Greatest Britons", a poll compiled by the British Broadcasting Corporation. He ranked 73rd, four places ahead of popstar Robbie Williams. In fact, making him the villain these days is more surprising than casting him as the hero. Like us all, I suspect he could be a little of both and rarely all of either.

Mathers was a contemporary (and they often did not see eye to eye). He did buy Boleskine in order to practice the Abramelin Ritual. He apparently summoned all manner of forces into existence and then, due to personal circumstances intruding, failed to complete the ritual and banish them. There are those who believe Crowley contaminated the house with evil in so doing. It's difficult to comment as, like Holmes, your own beliefs get in the way of assimilating the information. As a case in point: in a documentary on Crowley's time in Boleskine, paranormal writer (and author of *The Space Vampires* filmed by Tobe Hooper as *Lifeforce*, one of the finest bad movies ever made) Colin Wilson states unequivocally that Crowley discovered magic worked. I would qualify that as: "Crowley discovered magic worked for *him*" because I don't believe in magic (or, as Crowley always said, wishing to differentiate from stage illusion and Telstar romantic mail order LPs, *Magick*). But then I'm a rationalist who finds himself writing about things he doesn't believe in, the theme of the book as I'm sure you now realise.

2. FICTIONAL THEFT

So we come to the fictional characters that I have appropriated. Or, as some would say "nicked". The game of using old literary characters is not a new one and I hope that I have played by the rules by bringing something new and interesting to them (otherwise it's rather like a bland cover version, a waste of everyone's time).

Carnacki was the first to offer his services. I have long been a fan of William Hope Hodgson's original collection of nine stories. They offer innovative takes on haunting, though, as here, Carnacki sometimes finds that he has been presented with a hoax rather than a genuine example of the supernatural. If one thing is lacking in Hodgson's stories it's in the character of Carnacki himself. He is rather two-dimensional. It is fiction of ideas rather than personality. Hopefully I've altered that. I've also built up on a couple of Hodgson devices, the Electric Pentacle is more extensively described and used here than it ever was in the original. Other trimmings, the tattoos, cufflinks and affectation towards cookery are all my own.

Dr John Silence was created by Algernon Blackwood, whose weird writings were much enjoyed by the more famous HP Lovecraft. He is probably most well known for his story *The Willows*. In the sort of perfect twist authors love, Blackwood himself was a member of the Golden Dawn, albeit after Crowley's time. Like Carnacki, the character of Silence was secondary to a fiction of weird concepts and dream imagery. His animal companions, Smoke and Flame, do appear in the very first Silence story, *A Psychical Invasion*, though they are the real-live contemporaries of the elemental spirits seen to fight here.

Julian Karswell is the villain in the MR James story, *Casting the Runes*. He is a man singularly incapable of taking criticism (something I play with here) marking his literary enemies for death using scraps of paper with runes on them. James is the absolute master of the supernatural tale and I couldn't resist bringing a little of him here. The story Karswell tells of the maze in his home owes a debt to another James story, that of *Mr Humphreys and his Inheritance*. In this book, Karswell is played by actor Niall MacGinnis, who took on the role for the only big screen adaptation of a James story, 1957's *Night of the Demon* (*Curse of the Demon* in the US). The appearance of the demon in smoke during the Battle of Boleskine is also a nod to the movie, alongside a particularly cheeky joke I play with the dialogue. Fans of Kate Bush will spot the hidden reference.

I hope that any readers not familiar with these other stories will hunt them out. Hours of writing far superior to mine lie ahead of those that do. I also heartily recommend the audiobook recording of *Casting the Runes* by Andrew Sachs available from www.textbookstuff.com

3. THE CANON

Finally let's look at Holmes and Watson. There is a habit amongst writers of new Holmes fiction to concentrate on emulating Conan Doyle's style. From the word go I decided not to be too slavish about this. Guess what: Conan Doyle didn't write this, I did. That's not to say I didn't want to get the characters right and add a novel to the countless masses that I felt worthy of consideration, but I'm a storyteller not an impressionist. I wanted to write the sort of full-blooded romp that Conan Doyle would approve of (action and effect over logic and style if I'm unbearably honest). I also wanted to relish these two glorious leading men and enjoy them for all they were worth. They have brought me pleasure since I was a child and there's something quite breathtaking about getting to control them for a while.

Langdale Pike is also a creation of Conan Doyle's, though we never meet him. Here I have taken the liberty of imagining him to be personified by the wonderful Peter Wyngarde as was the case in Granada's TV adaptation of *The Three Gables* in 1994.

I have taken care to adhere to the character's chronology while allowing myself the odd self-indulgent joke at Conan Doyle's inconsistencies (the notion of Holmes, a man who loathed the countryside later retiring to keep bees, for example, the contradiction of which confused my noble editor no end). The fluctuating state of Watson's marriage is here given a more pleasing solidity, I wanted the man I cared for to be allowed the luxury to grieve. Nobody who has ever loved could fail to cheat him of that.

ACKNOWLEDGEMENTS

Sincere thanks to Titan Books in general and Cath Trechman in particular for letting me write this book. If it gives a reader half the pleasure it gave the writer... then I will have been ever so self-indulgent.

As always, it couldn't have been written without the help and support of my splendid family. Princess Loobrins read it and said she loved it while pointing me straight where needed. Old Ma Hudson thought it was the best thing I've ever written (which says more about her than me). Plucky pugilists and tearaways, Sharp Right Seph and Dunkin' Danny of the Arches asked how it was going when they really didn't have to. The Calle Gralla Irregulars: Smithers, Mango, Brins, Clive Owens, Ramsey, Martha, Bill, Skylark, Sheamus, Benjamin Franklin, Silent Singer, Lebowski, Udders and Nixie were no help at all.

Lastly, thanks to Sir Arthur Conan Doyle, for being a giant with shoulders broad enough for me to stand on.

About the Author

Guy Adams trained and worked as an actor for twelve years before becoming a full-time writer. He is the co-author of *The Case Notes of Sherlock Holmes*, and has written several tie-ins to the TV series *Life on Mars*. His most recently published novel is *Restoration*, the follow-up to the much-praised horror novel, *The World House*. To find out more visit his website: www.guy-adams.com.

PROFESSOR MORIARTY
THE HOUND OF THE D'URBERVILLES

Kim Newman

Imagine the twisted evil twins of Holmes and Watson and you have the dangerous duo of Professor James Moriarty—wily, snake-like, fiercely intelligent, terrifyingly unpredictable—and Colonel Sebastian 'Basher' Moran—violent, politically incorrect, debauched. Together they run London crime, owning police and criminals alike. When a certain Irene Adler turns up on their doorstep with a proposition, neither man is able to resist.

Praise for Kim Newman:

"Newman's prose is a delight." — *Time Out*

"A *tour de force* which succeeds brilliantly." — *The Times*

"Powerful... compelling entertainment..." — *San Francisco Chronicle*

"One of the most creative novels of the year." — *Seattle Times*

WWW.TITANBOOKS.COM

THE FURTHER ADVENTURES OF SHERLOCK HOLMES

Sir Arthur Conan Doyle's timeless creation returns in a series of handsomely designed detective stories. The Further Adventures of Sherlock Holmes encapsulates the most varied and thrilling cases of the world's greatest detective.

THE ECTOPLASMIC MAN
by Daniel Stashower

THE WAR OF THE WORLDS
by Manley Wade Wellman & Wade Wellman

THE SCROLL OF THE DEAD
by David Stuart Davies

THE STALWART COMPANIONS
by H. Paul Jeffers

THE VEILED DETECTIVE
by David Stuart Davies

THE MAN FROM HELL
by Barrie Roberts

SÉANCE FOR A VAMPIRE
by Fred Saberhagen

THE SEVENTH BULLET
by Daniel D. Victor

THE WHITECHAPEL HORRORS
by Edward B. Hanna

DR. JEKYLL AND MR. HOLMES
by Loren D. Estleman

THE ANGEL OF THE OPERA
By Sam Siciliano

THE GIANT RAT OF SUMATRA
by Richard L. Boyer

THE PEERLESS PEER
by Philip José Farmer

THE STAR OF INDIA
by Carole Buggé

COMING SOON:

THE WEB WEAVER
By Sam Siciliano

THE TITANIC TRAGEDY
By William Seil

WWW.TITANBOOKS.COM

ANNO DRACULA
KIM NEWMAN

It is 1888 and Queen Victoria has remarried, taking as her new consort Vlad Tepes, the Wallachian Prince infamously known as Count Dracula. His polluted bloodline spreads through London as its citizens increasingly choose to become vampires.

In the grim backstreets of Whitechapel, a killer known as 'Silver Knife' is cutting down vampire girls. The eternally young vampire Geneviève Dieudonné and Charles Beauregard of the Diogenes Club are drawn together as they both hunt the sadistic killer, bringing them ever closer to Britain's most bloodthirsty ruler yet.

"Compulsory reading... Glorious." — Neil Gaiman

"*Anno Dracula* is the definitive account of that post-modern species, the self-obsessed undead." — *The New York Times*

"*Anno Dracula* will leave you breathless... one of the most creative novels of the year." — *Seattle Times*

"Powerful... compelling entertainment... a fiendishly clever banquet of dark treats." — *San Francisco Chronicle*

WWW.TITANBOOKS.COM